controversy

ADRIANNE byrd

controversy

ARABESQUE®

CONTROVERSY

An Arabesque novel

ISBN-13: 978-0-373-83100-5
ISBN-10:   0-373-83100-5

www.kimanipress.com

Printed in U.S.A.

To the Byrd Watchers Book Club Group, thanks so much for your support. I hope this episode of the Adams sisters will continue to delight you.

Chapter 1

"I oughta kill him," Michael Adams grumbled into her third Long Island iced tea. "I gave that bastard the best years of my life. The least he could do is drop dead."

Michael's sisters, Peyton, Joey, Sheldon and Frankie sat huddled around Mike at their usual table in the Peppermill. Each of the sisters avoided making eye contact with their angry sister in hopes they wouldn't get dragged into some evil revenge plan inspired by her increasing amount of alcohol.

"C'mon, girls. You must agree with me," Mike said. She noticed the absence of amens to her latest rant and grew irritable about the lack of support.

Brave Sheldon, the eldest of the Adams clan, spoke up first. "You said we were going to celebrate your divorce being final. This is starting to feel more like a wake."

"We are celebrating!" Mike lifted her glass and egged her sisters on to join her in a toast.

The girls painted on smiles and lifted their glasses.

"To Philip's balls rotting off!" Mike barked.

The glasses came back down with a collective moan.

"I'm kidding. I'm kidding." Michael laughed. She held up her glass again and waited for the others to join her. "To new beginnings!"

"Hear! Hear!"

Everyone's glasses clinked together.

Michael gave her best effort to climb out of her two-year depression. A condition she thought she hid well; but tonight it was a lot harder than normal.

Divorced.

The word left a bitter taste in her mouth—one she kept hoping the vodka would wash off. So far, it wasn't working.

"Philip was having an affair," she blurted.

The sisters fell silent and darted cautionary glances around the table.

"Are you sure?" Peyton, the designated driver by default because she was eight months pregnant, set her ginger ale down and reached for Michael's hand. "Did he tell you this?"

"Don't be ridiculous." Mike rolled her eyes and reached for another nacho chip piled high with her favorite toppings. "Phil isn't bold enough to confess and he's too damn smart to get caught."

More darting gazes and Michael reached for another chip.

"Did you hire a private investigator?" Frankie asked, leaning forward and twirling her own huge diamond ring. "Or are you just working on a hunch?"

"Hell. I'm better than any damn P.I. and you know it."

"This is true," Joey said.

The other sisters bobbed their heads in agreement.

Michael straightened triumphantly. "I just wish I could've caught him in the act, but that man is slicker than a can of oil," she complained, thinking about her many solo covert operations during their trial separation. She'd followed her ex-husband across town and had pulled weekend stakeouts in her old neighborhood. Each time, she was busted by the ever-present geriatric Neighborhood Watch gang.

Admitting Phil had gotten the best of her and had managed to walk away to tell the tale got under her skin.

"If *you* couldn't catch him then maybe he wasn't having an affair," Sheldon suggested. "If for no other reason than the fact he's scared of you." She looked to the other sisters and then added, "We all are."

Tears glossed Michael's eyes as she fluttered a hand over her heart. "Thanks, Sheldon. What a nice thing to say."

A round of snickering ensued and Mike took it in stride. Well, she tried to anyway. Peyton leaned over and wrapped an arm around her waist. "Cheer up, Mikey. Phil lost the best thing that has ever happened to him. Remember what happened between Joey and Lawrence a couple of years ago?"

Of course she remembered. Everyone remembered—because Joey made it a point to tell anyone who would listen about how her ex-almost-fiancé had dumped her on Valentine's Day when she was expecting an engagement ring. Instead, the Beverly Hills plastic surgeon married a leggy, silicone-stuffed model slash D-listed actress who couldn't act her way out of a box.

In the end, getting dumped turned out to be the best thing that happened to Joey because it led her to meet and fall in love with her megasuccessful, A-list director husband, Ryan Donovan.

Mike smiled through a film of tears. "You're right!" Mike declared. "Screw Phil."

"That's our girl," Frankie said, beaming.

When Joey squeezed Michael's thick waist, she grew self-conscious about the near sixty pounds she'd gained in the last two years. A great many of them resulted from her depression. She'd tried dieting a few times, but that had turned into a madcap comedy. She'd go weeks eating nothing but salads and chicken, only to watch the numbers on the scale mock her efforts by not moving or creeping higher. Once, she'd join a gym, worked out like crazy and garnered the same results.

In the end, carbohydrates were the only things that soothed her. The more, the merrier.

"I know just how I'd like to do him in, too," Michael sulked, returning to her soapbox. When her sisters' weary eyes turned toward her, she ignored them and continued, "I'd like to bash him over the head and stuff him into the trunk of my car—*then* I'd drive him somewhere no one could hear him scream."

"Sounds like you've put a lot of thought into this," Frankie said, worried.

"Thought, hell. I've dreamed—no—*fantasized* about it," Michael confessed. "I'd tie him to a tree and beat him to a bloody pulp…but not until I got the name of that trick he dumped me for."

Sheldon drew a deep breath and nibbled on her bottom lip—a sign she was trying not to say something.

"What is it?" Michael asked. "Spit it out."

"Well—" Sheldon glanced at the other girls to judge whether they'd have her back. "I was just wondering if you've thought about, um, or considered *talking* to someone about…some of your issues."

"What issues?"

The table fell silent.

"You all think I have issues?"

Peyton shrugged. "One or two."

"Peyton James Adams, you take that back," Michael barked.

"Last name is Carver," she corrected. "And I will not. Come on. It's no secret you get a little crazy when you feel slighted. How many times have you been arrested for one of your revenge pranks?"

"I seem to remember having a few partners in crime sitting right next to me."

"We're too old for that stuff now," Frankie admonished.

"Really? Joey didn't think we were too old when we broke into her ex-fiancé's house last year and rigged the place."

"What?" Sheldon, Frankie and Peyton thundered and whipped their heads in Joey's direction.

"Ex-*almost*-fiancé," Joey corrected. "And that was supposed to be our little secret," she hissed.

Michael waved her off. "Right. Whenever I'm helping you guys, everything is gravy, but when I ask for a favor on a simple thing like *murder,* it's suddenly a big deal." She realized that didn't come out right, but she just waved her hand and said, "Whatever."

It took some time, but the subject drifted away from Mike's so-called "issues" and the even stickier subject of murder. It wasn't as though she really wanted to kill Phil; but if she did, her sisters, of all people, should've had her back—even if they still liked their ex-brother-in-law.

Happy hour morphed into social hour and then finally into a full-blown club scene. Michael waved to a few friends and flirted with even more strangers, but it was the sight of two old high-school and college buddies, Ray and Scott Damon, that put a smile on her face.

Well past her drinking limit, Michael allowed the cute twins to pump more alcohol into her system while they reminisced about old times and the innumerable pranks they'd pulled on their unsuspecting friends.

Michael lost track of the time and it was her sisters who finally busted up the private party and announced she'd had enough. It was time to go home.

"You keep your chin up," Ray said, lifting his shot glass in a final toast. "We got your back, buddy."

"Yeah," Scott concurred. "We'll be seeing you again…real soon."

"Aw," Michael cooed. "I love you guys."

"C'mon on, Mike," Joey said. "Let's get you home."

Michael jutted a thumb and winked. It was great seeing her old friends though she had long lost track of what they were talking about.

"Aren't those the Damon twins?" Peyton asked, helping Mike put on her jacket.

"Yep," Mike said. "Haven't seen them since you divorced their best buddy, Ricky."

"Then that's a good thing," Peyton sneered. "Those two are nothing but trouble."

Michael laughed. "Oh, they're harmless."

It was closing time. As Mike walked out to the car, she realized she'd eaten too little and drunk too much, and when she got into the back of Peyton's car, she threw up her beloved nachos all over the backseat.

"Great. Just great," Peyton mumbled, frowning at the mess.

"Oh, I feel much better now." Michael panted. She rolled onto her back and watched as Sheldon, mother of six, whipped out emergency baby wipes and went to town cleaning both Michael and the backseat of Peyton's car while they were still in the Peppermill's parking lot.

"Is she going to be all right?" Frankie asked somewhere in the vicinity.

I'm fine, Michael said inside her head, because opening her mouth suddenly required too much effort.

"Just drive with the windows rolled down," Joey suggested. "The cool air should be good for her."

"Someone is going have to come with me. I won't be able to get her into the house alone," Peyton said. "I have to be careful with the baby."

"I'll go with you," Frankie volunteered. "Hubby is still out of town. So it's just me and Lola again tonight," she said, referring to the teacup Yorkie she treated like it was her own flesh and blood.

"We'll all go," Sheldon declared. "Joey and I will follow you. Try not to drive with your foot pressed to the floorboard, P.J."

"I don't know what you mean," Peyton lied unconvincingly.

Michael snickered and four heads peered down at her.

"Well, it looks like she's still with us," Frankie said, brushing back strands of Michael's hair. "How're you doing, Mikey?"

Managing just a smile, Michael snuggled her left cheek against her sister's palm. It had been years since she'd allowed someone else to comfort her. Despite being the middle child of five girls and a baby brother, Michael had always taken the leadership role in the family.

Everyone depended on her—not the other way around. But tonight, she told herself, just this once, she wanted someone else to take over before she fell apart.

"Oh, she'll sleep like a baby tonight." Joey laughed.

"Tonight's not the problem. Tomorrow morning is what she should be worried about," P.J. said.

Michael drew a deep breath, closed her eyes and welcomed her black oblivion—a place where nothing could harm her. Too bad she couldn't stay there forever. Even in her drunken state, she understood by morning she would have a splitting headache, an upset stomach and her cold porcelain toilet would be her best friend.

How pathetic.

What was more pathetic was to be thirty-eight and single again.

Single.

No children.

No career.

Nothing.

The realization brought fresh tears to the surface and rolled down the sides of her face. Was it so hard for a man to love her? Sure, she was strong willed and more than a handful, but whatever happened to the adage that there was someone for everyone?

Even her.

Were there no more tall, black knights who could step up to the plate and love her the way she yearned to be loved? If it could happen for her sisters, why couldn't it happen for her?

She groaned and opened her eyes. She wasn't interested in the conversation going on in the front seat between Peyton and Frankie; but while lying down, she stared out the back window and up at a blanket of stars twinkling against black velvet. It was a beautiful, clear night. The kind made for lovers.

Suddenly, a star shot across the night sky. Michael, feeling like a lost fairy princess, closed her eyes and made a wish and promptly fell into a deep sleep.

Chapter 2

For the first time in months, Michael enjoyed an erotic dream—and with someone other than her ex-husband. In fact, she didn't know who the mysterious dark-chocolate, hard-muscled man in her dreams was, and honestly, she didn't care. She just loved the way his nice, firm butt pumped and gyrated between her legs, causing her to inch up a large fantasy bed covered in black satin.

The heat this man generated had Michael kicking the sheets off her real bed and made every sensitive part of her body tingle and throb. As the dream stretched on, Mr. Fantasy tossed and flipped her into positions that would, in real life, require a team of engineers to pull off.

Damn, they were having a good time.

The bed started jumping and banging against the floor.

Michael's head tossed among the pillows as she drew toward her dramatic crescendo. The banging grew louder and somehow seemed out of sync with the wild sex performing in her head.

Then the banging became a distraction and she wanted whatever it was to stop.

It wouldn't.

Instead, it caused the throbbing between her legs to cease and her temples to hammer.

Someone was at the door, trying to break it down from the sounds of it.

Michael flopped over in the bed and buried her head beneath the pillows.

Still her insistent tormentor pounded away and made it clear that he/she/it wasn't going away anytime soon.

"Fine. I'm coming. I'm coming," she grumbled. Sitting up, she raked her acrylic nails through her hair before swinging her legs over the side of the bed. When she stood up, her scratching went from her head to her belly and then legs while she stepped over piles of clothes, books and whatnot.

She really did need to clean the place up and try to make it look like someone actually lived there.

When she finally neared the door, the pounding felt like a jackhammer against her skull and she swore if someone wasn't dead or dying, she would personally kill the SOB for waking her up at this hour.

Hell, what time was it?

"Who is it?" she snapped, ready to give whoever it was a *big* piece of her mind.

"Police! Open up!"

At the authoritative bark, Michael's hands stilled on the top lock. She was suddenly completely sober. A million questions raced through her mind while fear clogged her throat. By the time she turned all the locks and swung the door open, she was in a state of panic.

The first shock was that she recognized the man on the other side of the door as the dark-chocolate fantasy that had just been screwing her brains out upstairs in her dreams.

"Mrs. Michelle Matthews?" the sinfully deep baritone asked. His sharp onyx gaze impaled her.

"Michael," she corrected him hoarsely. Was she still dreaming? Would she invite this *cop* inside her house only for him to start a striptease in the living room that would lead her to being handcuffed to the bedposts?

God, she hoped so.

"Michelle Michaels?" He glanced down at his small pocket notepad.

"No. It's Michael Matthews—well, it was. It's

now Michael Adams," she rambled. "I'm divorced. Recently. Happily—sort of."

He frowned, his gaze traveling from the top of her hair, which she suspected was standing straight up from its roots, to the tips of her chip-painted toenails.

"Your name is Michael?"

"Friends and family call me Mikey or Mike."

His gaze returned to her figure, this time paying particular attention to her voluptuous curves.

She rolled her eyes. "Yes. I *am* a woman." His powerful gaze traveled back to her face and warmed it considerably.

"Yes, ma'am. You most certainly are."

The compliment took her by surprise and him, too, judging by how quickly his eyes diverted back to his notepad.

"I'm Detective Kyson Dekker and this is my partner, Detective Robert Griffin." He indicated a lanky white cop in black jeans and a T-shirt.

Up until that moment, Michael hadn't noticed the flaxen-haired detective. She gave him a cursory nod and then dismissed him to stare at this fantasy man.

"Is there a problem?" she asked, anxious again about why they were there and why they'd been about to break down her door.

"Yes, um." Dekker cleared his throat as he crossed his arms in a V in front of his body, planted his legs wide and darted his eyes around her own.

The man might as well have socked her in the

gut; his sudden change in demeanor confirmed he carried bad news.

"It's one of my sisters, isn't it?"

"Um, no, ma'am. We—"

"My baby brother?" But wait. He's in Georgia.

"No, ma'am. We—"

She gasped. "My father! It has to be my father. What was it—heart attack? Stroke? I told him about mixing that Viagra with his heart medication. But he never listens."

Detective Dekker's frown deepened. "No. That's *not* it."

"Stepmother? Though I'm not too crazy about her. I'd call her a gold digger if my father had any money," she added absently. "No one knows that much about her, she just popped up—"

"Ms. Matthews—"

"Adams."

"Right," he snapped with impatience.

She caught the underlying hint and shut up—but, damn, he was fine.

"Ms. *Adams,* we're here regarding your husband—"

"Ex-husband."

He drew a deep breath. "Right. Mr. Matthews is missing and his, ah, lady friend suspects foul play. She suggested we come and talk to you."

Lady friend? "I knew it." She swore under her breath. "I'll kill him."

Detective Dekker's brows jumped and crinkled his forehead.

Embarrassment burned Michael's face. "I'm sorry. Figure of speech. You were saying?"

Dekker glanced over his shoulder at his partner and then returned his attention to Michael. "Ma'am, do you mind if we come in?"

It was Michael's turn to glance back over her shoulder and assess her pigsty of a house. Why, oh, why hadn't she cleaned up?

"Ma'am?"

"Um…sure." Reluctantly, she stepped back, pulling the door with her and allowing the two officers to enter.

Kyson crossed the threshold and made a sweeping glance around the quaint, although cluttered, house.

"I just moved in," she said.

"Yes, ma'am. Um, like I was saying, Mr. Matthews's place of residence appears to have been ransacked pretty badly, so our department concurs with Ms. Delaney's assessment and believes there's foul play at work here." He walked farther into the house, not sure what to make of the place.

Delaney—probably a hooker. "I'm sure I don't know what you mean," she said, closing the door behind Dekker's partner.

Grudgingly, Kyson returned his attention to the striking beauty, despite the bed-tossed hair, smudged makeup and mismatched plaid and polka-dot pajamas. The woman must've had one hell of a night.

"Ma'am," Griffin said when Dekker couldn't stop staring, "can you tell us where you were last night?"

"Yes. With my sisters. We went out for drinks at the Peppermill."

"All night?" Kyson asked, his voice returning.

"Until it closed," she said. "We were out celebrating."

Kyson lifted an inquisitive brow.

"My divorce," she answered the unasked question. "It was made final yesterday," she supplied.

Kyson reached for his pen and flipped open his notepad again. "And your sisters will verify this?"

"Yes," she clipped with a hint of anger.

"Their names?" Griffin asked.

"Sheldon, Frankie, Joey and Peyton."

Kyson glanced at his partner.

"Yes. Yes. We all have boy names. Next subject."

"What time did you return home?"

She shrugged. "I have no idea. I passed out in the backseat of my sister's car. They put me to bed and I didn't wake until you guys started pounding down the door. For which, by the way, if there are any damages, I'll be suing the department."

The partners exchanged weary looks.

"When was the last time you spoke to or heard from your husband?"

Her eyes narrowed.

"Excuse me," Kyson said. "Your *ex*-husband."

"I don't know." She shrugged again. "A week ago—maybe two."

"Ms. Delaney says you were stalking Mr. Matthews," Griffin tossed in. "Any truth to that?"

"Absolutely not!" she shouted, but then followed it up with, "I was spying on him."

Kyson suspected someone had spiked his morning coffee—either that or he'd stepped into the twilight zone.

"You weren't stalking, you were spying?" Griffin asked with his pen poised above his notepad, just like Kyson's.

The woman nodded. "I suspected he was having an affair, but I couldn't catch him. I take it that this *Ms. Delaney* is his elusive ho."

Kyson chuckled.

"Ms. Delaney just identified herself as 'a friend,'" Griffin informed her.

"Uh-huh," she said, crossing her arms and rolling her eyes.

"Do you mind if we sit down and ask you a few more questions?" Kyson asked, not ready to leave.

She considered the question and then shrugged again as if to say "why not?"

He and Griffin followed behind her as she led the way to the living room. Kyson's eyes locked on the way her hips rolled and her butt swayed with every step she took. She was the kind of woman Southern men like him would just sop up with a biscuit and suck on the bones for a few hours.

"Would you like some coffee?" she asked.

"No," Griffin said, casing the room.

"I'd love some," Kyson contradicted, mainly because he wanted to see her walk some more.

She caught on; but instead of calling him on it, she flashed him a smile. Two dimples winked back before she disappeared into the kitchen.

Kyson's heart jumped while his erection pressed against the line of his pants. He needed to sit down.

"So what do you think?" Griffin whispered. "You think she's hiding something?"

"Don't know," he answered, and took a seat.

"She's sort of an odd bird, don't you think?" Griffin asked. "When she opened the door, I thought we'd arrived at Pee-wee's Playhouse. Plaid and polka dots?"

Kyson's mouth curled. "I saw that and then some," he said, remembering the sight of her overflowing breasts. She certainly had more than a handful. He licked his lips. His mouth was dry as a desert.

Griffin chuckled. "Didn't know you had a thing for crazy women."

"They keep life interesting."

Michael searched all of the cupboards and cabinets and came up empty. Just her luck. She was out of coffee. An amazingly gorgeous man was in her house and she couldn't even offer him a decent cup of coffee.

"Maybe there's some downstairs," she muttered.

Last week, Michael's father had given her boxes of canned food and whatnot from his overflowing Costco stock. There had to be some coffee down there.

"Just a minute, guys." Michael exited the kitchen with a pasted-on smile and raced to the door leading down to the basement. "Make yourselves comfortable, I have to get a new can of coffee."

"That's okay, ma'am," Detective Dekker said. "We don't want to put you through any trouble."

"No trouble," she lied. "Be back in a moment." Michael took off down the stairs. "C'mon, girl. Get it together," she coached. If she played her cards right, she might get Detective Fine's phone number. She clicked on a light.

"Where the hell did all this mud come from?" Michael glanced around and noticed the back door cracked open. "What in the hell?" She went and closed it. "Just more work that needs to be done," she mumbled and made a beeline to the piles of boxes from her father.

"Coffee. Coffee. Where's the coffee?" She dug through the canned goods and spotted the familiar burgundy canister. "Gotcha!" She smiled.

Pivoting on her heels, her gaze scanned across the basement and crashed into a horrific sight.

She jumped, screamed and dropped the can of coffee.

There, sitting before a cinder-block wall, looking bruised and battered, not to mention, tied in a wooden chair with his mouth duct taped, was her missing ex-husband, Philip Matthews.

Chapter 3

Remembering the cops upstairs in her living room, Michael clamped a hand over her mouth, but continued to stare wide-eyed at the angry face of her ex-husband. What in the hell did she do last night?

Phil rocked and bucked in this chair. No doubt his mumbled words behind his taped mouth were a long fervid stream of expletives and, given the circumstances, she didn't blame him. A lean five foot ten with hair shaved so low one would question whether to call it hair at all was still neatly groomed, but one would not miss the ugly purple-and-blue bruise against his left temple or the trickle of blood from his lips. His sable-brown eyes were wild and angry.

Again, she didn't blame him.

Michael stomped over to a squirming Phil and ripped the duct tape from his mouth.

"Ow!"

"What the hell are you doing here?"

His eyes rounded incredulously. "What does it look like?" he hissed. "I finally decided to take a vacation and spend it tied up in your basement."

"Ms. Adams?" Detective Dekker's voice floated down and filled the basement. "Do you need any help down there?"

Phil filled his lungs with air, but before he could yell for help, the duct tape was back wrapped around his mouth and she clamped her hand over it for good measure and plopped down into his lap to prevent him from bucking and rocking the chair.

"Uh, no. I have everything under control."

"You're sure?" The top stair creaked, letting her know that he was about to come down. "I thought I heard you scream."

"Rats!" she shouted, and cut her gaze back to her ex. "I seem to have a rat infestation. I'm on my way back up." With her free hand, she reached for the roll of duct tape on a cluttered shelf.

Dekker paused. "Are you sure you don't need help?"

"Positive." She waited.

And waited.

Then finally she heard his weight shift on the

stairs. Thinking he was about to descend, her heart plunged to her toes and all she could see in her mind was Detective Dekker slapping handcuffs on her wrists and sending her off to spend the rest of her life behind bars. Wasn't kidnapping, like, a federal offense?

For whatever reason, God had mercy on her soul and the cop went back upstairs and closed the door.

"Mmphf. Mmmugh," Phil muttered behind his sealed lips.

"Oh, shut up!" she snapped, removing her hand from his mouth. "I can't think with you doing all of that."

He glowered.

"What?" she challenged. "Just because I don't remember what happened last night doesn't mean that you didn't deserve it."

Phil shook his head and rolled his eyes. Undoubtedly, he was thinking that she'd finally snapped and lost her mind. Actually, it looked as if she had. Michael glanced down. She had a lot of questions, but she didn't take the tape back off because she didn't trust him not to shout for help.

"I'm sorry about this," she said. A half truth, but she would examine that later. Right now, she took the roll of tape and wrapped so much of it around his head his eyes bulged. "I'll be right back."

Michael raced out of the basement and up the stairs. She had to get those cops out of her house quick, fast and in a hurry, but she was at a loss as to how she could do that without raising suspicions.

When she rushed into the living room, she was stunned to see Frankie and Sheldon there, shaking hands with the officers and smiling a little too openly at her dream lover.

Heifers.

Four sets of eyes swiveled in her direction. She told the first lie that came to mind. "Looks like I'm out of coffee."

Frankie frowned. "All that coffee Daddy packed up for you?"

"Well, I couldn't find it," she said through clenched teeth.

"Don't be ridiculous," Frankie insisted, heading for the basement door. "I helped him pack the cans myself."

"Don't go down there!" Michael barked, jumping in front of her sister.

"What in the hell?" Frankie leaped back and stared at her sister as if she'd grown two heads. "What's gotten into you?"

The detectives stared at them.

Michael laughed to defuse the situation. She needed to step up her game. She was usually cooler under pressure, but something about being under Dekker's close scrutiny frayed her nerves.

"Um, I, uh—there's, um…" *Calm down, Mike.*

Calm down. "Rats!" She remembered. "Big. Huge. Rats. Trust me. You don't want to go down there."

"I guess we're going have to skip out on the coffee anyway," Detective Griffin said. "Your sisters here corroborate your story."

"Rats?" Sheldon echoed, looking over Michael's shoulder and toward the door.

"Yeah," Dekker added with a soft smirk. "Sounds like you got pretty lit last night."

"Speaking of which," Frankie said, reaching into her expensive bag. "P.J. sent you this bill for her having to have the car cleaned."

"Figures." Michael snatched the bill from her hand.

"Maybe we need to get the exterminators here," Sheldon said, still frowning at the door. "If the problem is really bad, maybe it's not too late to get you out of the lease." She sidestepped Michael.

Michael blocked her again. "Trust me. You don't want to go down there."

"Oh, I'm not afraid of rodents." She shoved Mike out of the way. "If this is a serious problem then we need to jump on it."

There was nothing else to do but to watch Sheldon plow through the door. "You coming, Frankie?"

Frankie laughed as if to say "get real" and turned her attention back to the cops. "I'm sure Phil is fine," she assured them. "While he and Michael were married, he had a habit of disappearing. Isn't that right, Mike?"

"Uh?" Mike tore her gaze from the door, lost in what was being said.

"Phil," Frankie stressed.

Michael panicked. "What about him? I don't know where he is!"

Frankie frowned.

Sheldon bolted back through the door with wide, wild eyes, and slammed it behind her.

"What the hell?" Frankie asked, turning.

Michael quickly moved to Sheldon's side. "I told you not to go down there," she said.

"My goodness." Frankie joined her sisters by the door. "Is it that bad?"

Sheldon panted as if she'd run a marathon. Her shocked gaze swung from Michael to the two officers.

"Ma'am? Are you all right?"

Michael jumped in before Sheldon spilled her guts. "I take it you saw the big *rat* downstairs?"

"Rat?" she echoed.

Michael swore if she was hauled to jail she'd strangle Sheldon first before they carted her off.

"Rat!" Sheldon affirmed, nodding, finally catching on. "Huge. We need to, uh, get someone here quick to, um, handle it." She swallowed.

"Damn." Frankie glanced around. "If they're down there, they can be up here, as well." In dramatic fashion, Frankie leaped up onto the leather couch. "I'm allergic to rodents."

Michael shook her head at her sister's diva-esque

tendency. They'd all grown up digging in the dirt and climbing trees, but ever since Frankie married up, she acted as if she was born and raised in Beverly Hills.

"Maybe I should check it out for you," Dekker suggested.

"No!" Michael and Sheldon shouted, both crowding and blocking the door.

Detective Dekker jerked back, but then his eyebrows crashed together.

"It's already dead," Sheldon lied to cover.

Michael nodded, unable to speak. She was too busy praying for another miracle.

A phone chirped and Detective Griffin reached into his jacket while Detective Dekker reached into his back pocket.

This is it. I'm about to be handcuffed and dragged out of here in my pajamas like an episode of Cops.

Instead, Detective Dekker produced a business card. Cops had business cards?

"If you do see or hear from your husband—"

"Ex."

He smiled and amended, "Ex-husband, please don't hesitate to give us a call. My cell phone number is on the back."

One miracle delivered.

"Thanks," Michael said, taking the offered card and slipping it into her pajamas top and down her bra. "If I hear anything you're on the top of my list."

Kyson didn't hear a word she said. His attention was focused on that lucky card he'd passed her. He'd watched the whole thing as if it played in slow motion.

"I don't see what the big deal is," Frankie interjected. "No body. No crime."

"We gotta roll," Griffin said, cutting into Kyson's X-rated thoughts. "We have a new lead."

When Kyson didn't respond, he walked over and clamped a hand down on his partner's shoulder. "Let's go." Griffin chuckled. "One of Matthews's neighbors called, said she thought she'd seen something suspicious this morning. Thinks she got a good look at a car peeling out of the neighborhood."

That damn Neighborhood Watch gang, Michael thought.

Kyson nodded and then returned his attention to the unique and unusual Michael Adams. "Make sure you use that card," he said. It was the only thing he could say without spelling it out to her that he *wanted* her to call whether it was in regard to her missing ex-husband or not.

Griffin muttered something beneath his low laugh and then led the way back to the front door. The Adams sisters followed.

"Could you be any more pathetic?" Griffin asked when they climbed into Griff's late-model Mercury Sable.

"What?" Kyson laughed, though he knew exactly what his partner meant. He had acted like a teenager with a crush on his high-school teacher.

Griff shook his head and started the car. "I don't know, Kyson. You need to leave this one alone. Something tells me Ms. Adams eats men like you for breakfast."

"You say that like it's a bad thing."

Chapter 4

Sheldon and Michael crouched by the door and watched as the officers climbed into their vehicle. It seemed like it was taking forever for Detective Griffin to start the car.

"Can I ask what the hell you two are doing?" Frankie asked, standing behind them.

"Shh," they hissed over their shoulders, their eyes glued to the car.

The engine started. Michael and Sheldon reached for each other's hands and held their breaths while the car backed out of the driveway. The short paved slab suddenly seemed a mile long.

Annoyed to be left out of the loop, Frankie

inched up and crowded around the thin, glass panes next to the front door. Still she was clueless why they were watching the cops leave the property.

"That Detective Dekker was cute," she hazarded a guess as to what the big deal was. "He'd make a good rebound guy."

No response.

Frankie rolled her eyes.

The cop car pulled off from the property and Sheldon jumped as if a bomb had exploded beneath her.

"Michael Anthony Adams, you have lost your mind!" She snatched her hand away, bolted from the door and raced through the house.

"I can explain," Michael lied, dogging her heels.

Frankie took up the rear, still clueless. "Somebody tell me what's going on!"

"We're going to jail!" Sheldon shouted as she threw open the basement door and flew down the stairs. "My children are going to grow up without a mother because I have a crazy sister!"

"Stop being dramatic," Michael said, determined to downplay the situation.

"What about the rats?" Frankie asked, slowing as she descended the stairs. "Shouldn't we wait until we call the exterminator?"

"There are no rats!" Sheldon shouted. She rounded the corner and skidded to a stop as if she'd

"Don't!" Michael shouted. She was nowhere near ready to go to jail…again.

"We can't leave him tied up down here," Frankie reasoned, cradling her bejeweled hands against her hips. "I love you, but I'm not about to become an accessory after the fact. I happen to *love* my freedom."

"And I don't?" Michael stepped forward, ready to direct her anger at someone else. Anyone, really, would do. "Why should I go to jail for something I don't remember doing? For all I know, he tied himself up down here."

Everyone kept their incredulous eyes on her.

"Well," she said, annoyed no one bought that outrageous possibility. "It could've happened," Michael insisted.

"Phil is right," Frankie said. "You're psycho!"

"Now *you* take that back!"

"Make me!" Frankie stepped forward.

"Girls, girls!" Sheldon planted herself between the sisters. "Everyone needs to just calm down and take a deep breath."

Michael took several, but it did nothing to calm her nerves or steady her heartbeat. Over the years, she'd prided herself on getting out of some pretty sticky situations, but now she feared she'd finally landed in something she wouldn't be able to get out of.

"Just tell us what happened," Sheldon continued in the same calming voice.

Michael closed her eyes and tried to remember,

but the only images that would come were snippets of her laughing and drinking at the Peppermill, vomiting in Peyton's car and staring up at the blanket of stars while lying in the backseat.

"I don't remember," she finally said. Her shoulders slumped with despair. "But I know I was in no condition to pull off a kidnapping. You girls know that."

Sheldon and Frankie reluctantly agreed.

"But you were apparently able to hire two thugs to do your dirty work," Phil cut in snidely. Anger still simmered in his eyes.

Sheldon and Frankie groaned; their support shifted back into Phil's court.

"I'll tell you what happened," Phil spat. "I had just come home from working late at the office—"

"Geez, we're not even married anymore and you're still using that same tired excuse?"

"I. Was. Working," he insisted, eyes blazing.

Michael made a dismissive wave. "Whatever."

Sheldon and Frankie rolled their eyes.

Phil cleared his throat. "Now, where was I?"

"You just came home after *working,*" the women repeated dully.

"Right." He cleared his throat. "I went upstairs to take a shower, but just as I walked into my bedroom—"

"Our bedroom," Michael couldn't help but correct him.

"*You* don't live there anymore."

"It's still part mine until the property is sold."

Phil opened his mouth to respond, when Sheldon jumped in. "Are you two kidding me? You two are divorced. Michael, will you please let him finish this story before my hundredth birthday?"

Phil flashed a smug smile.

Michael stuck her tongue out at him.

"What is this—*Romper Room?*" Frankie snapped.

Thoroughly chastised, Michael crossed her arms, clamped her jaw shut and grudgingly let Phil finish his story.

"So," Phil went on. "I walked into *my* bedroom and before I could flip on the light switch your two goons slipped a pillowcase over my head and proceeded to beat the living *crap* out of me!"

A genuine smile eased across Michael's face. "Now, *that* I wish I was around to see."

"Michael," Sheldon warned, and then returned her attention to Phil. "What men?"

"How the hell would I know?" he said defensively. "Men—her cronies. All dressed in black and threatening to cut off my..." He coughed and cleared his throat. "Threatening to hurt me if I didn't come with them."

The sisters stared.

"So you went with them?" Frankie asked, trying to speed along the story.

"Like I had a choice." Phil's hard gaze swung from Mike to Frankie. "After the largest man used my chest as a punching bag for a few rounds, it was more like they carried me out."

"This is crazy!" Michael barked. "I didn't send any men over to rough him up or kidnap him," she pleaded to her sisters.

Sheldon rolled her eyes. "And yet, here he is tied up in *your* basement." She returned her attention to Phil. "Continue."

"What else is there to say? I was clubbed over the head and dragged here. And now the three of you refuse to untie me."

"We're not refusing," Frankie snapped, but made no move to release him. "We're carefully weighing our options."

"Where do I come in on this incredible story?" Michael asked. "I didn't know you were here until I came down for some coffee."

"Tell it to a jury," Phil said. "Now, untie me!"

No one made a move.

"Now!" he roared.

"Can you put the tape back over his mouth so we can think?" Mike asked.

Frankie complied, but not without muttering, "Sorry about this."

"No. Wait. No." Phil tried twisting his head, but Frankie successfully rewound the duct tape around his mouth.

Mike still couldn't conjure a defense to Phil's allegations.

"What's this?" Frankie asked, removing something pinned to Phil's filthy blue shirt.

Michael and Sheldon quickly crowded around while Phil went back to mumbling behind his sealed lips and bouncing in his wooden chair.

"Oh, simmer down." Michael popped him on the back of the head. The man really could be annoying at times. "Who's it from?" she asked, returning her attention to the letter.

"'Dear Mikey,'" Frankie read. "'After seeing you so depressed last night at the Peppermill, Ray and I thought you had a killer idea on how to exact revenge on your ex.'"

"Ray?" Michael said, bouncing the name in her mind, but coming up empty. Hell, she still hadn't had her morning coffee.

Frankie continued, "'By the way, I never liked your ex personally. I always thought you could do better. You should have seen him crying for his momma when we picked him up.'"

The sisters swung their eyes toward Phil.

"'Ray has it all on his camera phone. Funny stuff.'"

Michael laughed. "Looks like I will get to see it."

Frankie read on, "'No need to thank us, we figured this would make us even for when you helped us get revenge on a certain fraternity back in college. Good times, huh? We roughed him up a bit, but it was all in good fun.'"

"See? There's nothing in there that says I had anything to do with this."

"'Your directions to the house were great,'" Frankie read.

"What?" Michael sputtered and then glanced around at the hostile crowd. "All right…" She stalled while trying to think of something to say. "Maybe…I mentioned where I used to live." She shrugged. "It doesn't mean I told them to break in."

Frankie read the next line. "'You were right. Your husband hadn't gotten around to changing the security codes and we walked right in.'"

Sheldon groaned and looked around. "I need to sit down."

Michael stubbornly clung to denial. "I did *not* tell them to kidnap Phil."

Again Frankie read. "'You're an evil genius, Mikey. Your plan went off without a hitch.'"

"Give me that." Michael snatched the letter from her sister's hands and read the damning words for herself and then quoted the last line. "'Give him hell, doll! Your faithful friends, the Damon twins.'"

"More like the *Demon* twins," Sheldon said, and then added, "Well, it looks like we're going to jail."

Chapter 5

Kyson tried to concentrate on his job. Truly he did, but during the ride back to Phil Matthews's neighborhood, his mind looped footage of Michael Adams answering her front door. She'd looked either sexy or crazy—or maybe even a little of both, depending on your preference.

He, for one, found the combination fascinating. She was also older—another thing he found attractive. Lately, he had a penchant for older ladies. The closely guarded secret being older women were cougars in the bedroom—and if she was a thick girl, too? Lawd, have mercy.

Kyson sucked in a breath and rolled his eyes

skyward at the possibility of reaching heaven in Michael Adams's arms.

"You're still thinking about that chick, aren't you?" Griff asked, chuckling while he parked.

Instead of answering, Kyson climbed out of the car and strolled up the paved driveway with the sound of his partner's laughter trailing him.

After two quick raps on the door of 519 Hillendale Drive, the partners put on their game faces and waited for the door to open. There was a long wait; but when it finally did open, only a partial view of the left side of an elderly woman's face could be seen.

"What do you want?" a quivering rumble snapped.

Griffin flipped opened his notepad and inquired, "Ms. Juanita Perkins?"

"Who wants to know?"

Kyson and Griffin drew deep breaths.

Kyson took over. "Ms. Perkins, I'm Detective Dekker and this is my partner, Detective Griffin. You called reporting a disturbance?"

"You the police?"

"Yes, ma'am," Kyson answered, still mystified by her behavior. One would think she lived in the middle of Compton instead of in the hub of suburban paradise.

"Show me your badges," she barked.

The two detectives followed her command and waited to be granted permission to enter the premises.

"How do I know those are real?"

Was she serious?

"Ma'am, you called us—not the other way around," Griff snapped, his patience for BS nearing its end.

There was a grunt before she slammed the door. Seconds passed like minutes and the cops shared a careless shrug and turned around.

The door swung open.

"Are you guys coming in here or what?"

Old or not, the woman was riding Kyson's last nerve. However, when he turned back around, he was stunned to see someone who was only tall enough to reach his hip.

The partners strolled into the house, but nearly tumbled back out when the harsh scent of Ben-Gay singed their nose hairs.

What did the lady do, use a whole tube?

Griff rudely fanned the air around him.

"What took you so long to get here?" she snapped, slamming the door again. "I've been calling the station all morning."

Kyson walked past a stool and guessed that was what she'd stood on when she'd opened the door. "Sorry, ma'am. We just received word of your call a few minutes ago." He glanced around and wondered if the woman would take offense if he was to suggest they crack a window open.

"Mmm-hmm," she said in a tone of disbelief and began a slow creep toward the living room.

The partners surmised that they were supposed to follow. "Ma'am, if you could just tell us what you saw last night…"

"Hold your breeches, young man," she snapped. "We've waited all morning for you, you can at least extend us the same courtesy."

"Us?" Kyson repeated just as he entered the living room and saw a small circle of five elderly women nestled in upholstery furniture, crowded with throw pillows.

"Did we interrupt an AARP meeting or something?" Griff whispered, coming up behind Kyson.

"Ha. Ha," Ms. Perkins said, sounding anything but amused. "The white one is a regular Rodney Dangerfield," she informed the group.

The women's eyes narrowed and successfully wiped the cocky smile from Griffin's lips.

"I may be old, honey, but there's nothing wrong with my hearing," Ms. Perkins chastised as she made it to her seat on the sofa's last cushion. "You young folks today need to learn to respect your elders."

Kyson and Griff stood before the ring of women, feeling as if they'd just been caught stealing cookies out of the cookie jar.

Apparently feeling she'd made her point, Juanita Perkins pulled a crocheted blanket over her lap and then reached for her teacup and saucer from the table next to her.

After a beat of silence, Kyson cleared his throat. "Good afternoon, ladies. We apologize for not responding to your call sooner, but my partner and I were chasing down other leads. I hope you can forgive us."

Ms. Perkins finally cracked a smile—a small one, but at least it was a start.

"Well, you gentlemen are looking at the best Neighborhood Watch in the country."

Griff lifted a curious brow. "Is that right?"

"Yes, that's right." The smile vanished from Juanita's face. "You know I don't like your condescending tone. We run a tip-top shift in this neighborhood. Isn't that right, Estelle?"

"It most certainly is," the only white woman in the pack, with hair so white it looked like a fluffy ball of cotton, said. "We know everything that goes on in this block." As if offering proof, she brandished a walkie-talkie just as it chirped to life.

"Mr. Ellison has just left the premises to walk his dog. Looks like he finally heeded our warnings to put a leash on that wild beast. Maybe it will keep that four-legged freak out of your prized flower bed, Estelle. Over."

Estelle smiled in triumph. "He better or I'll clip the dog's balls off myself." She returned the walkie-talkie to her lap. "Ferocious animal."

"What kind of dog is it?" Kyson asked.

"Chihuahua. Barks like the dickens."

Kyson didn't know how he managed to keep a straight face. "Can we get back to why you called the station?"

The six ladies nodded.

"So who wants to go first?"

"I will," Juanita stated proudly. "I was awakened at precisely 2:12 a.m."

"How are you so sure about the time?" Griff asked, cutting her off.

"I looked at the clock," she answered as if she dealt with a simpleton.

"Right," Griffin said at the obvious answer. "Please continue."

Ms. Perkins drew an impatient breath, but went on with her story. "I woke up at precisely 2:12 a.m. when I heard a loud bang."

"A bang?"

"Well, maybe it was more like a thump," she said, drumming a finger against her chin.

Kyson closed his eyes and counted to ten.

"Anyway, my bedroom window faces the Matthewses' residence—at least the driveway and the carport area—and what I heard was someone running over the Matthewses' empty garbage can. It's plastic—sort of like that Rubbermaid material."

"We've told Philip about leaving the container out," Estelle cut in.

"That's right," Juanita concurred. "Everyone is

supposed to roll their garbage cans back from the curbside the same day the garbagemen empty them."

"You know," Estelle leaped in again. "For curb appeal."

"Uh-huh," Kyson said, suspecting that he was not only talking to an overzealous Neighborhood Watch but also the Home Owners' Association group.

"Of course, we're pretty lenient with folks. You know, sometimes if you are going to be away for some reason. An extended vacation, one of us will be more than happy to make sure the plastic receptacles are rolled back for you."

"That is very…kind of you."

"Yes, well." Juanita cleared her throat. "Well, the Matthewses have been sort of a problem since they moved into the neighborhood."

"Not Phil," a new woman corrected. "Oh, by the way, I'm Louise."

Kyson gave her a nod in greeting. He, and apparently no one else, hadn't the heart to tell Louise her wig was seriously off center.

"Oh, no. Phil is a sweetheart," Juanita agreed. "It's *her* that was always the problem."

"Her?" Kyson questioned, but he already knew to whom they referred.

"Yes. *Her.*" Louise straightened. "*Mrs.* Matthews."

"Ex-Mrs. Matthews," Juanita corrected. "She evidently thought the rules didn't apply to her. One year she painted the shutters this horrible cotton-candy pink and then had the nerve to install a chain-link fence instead of the Home Owners' Association-approved *private* fence. Ugh!" Juanita tossed up her hands. "Just thinking about the daily battles we had with that…that…woman is enough to spike my blood pressure."

Another club member piped in. "One time, she installed a vulgar mailbox of a man bent over, poking his bum out. Every time the mailman opened the mailbox, essentially he was pulling the man's pants down."

The circle of women groaned as if they remembered the horrific event clearly.

"And when there were envelopes ready to pick up," the woman went on, "it looked like…like…"

"We got the picture," Kyson said, saving her from having to complete the sentence. However, he couldn't stop the subtle smile curving his lips.

"Anyway," Juanita said, seizing control of the conversation, "when I heard the thump, I looked at the clock and then grabbed my glasses because I can't see a thing without them."

The circle of women nodded as if they could all testify to the statement.

"Once I got those on, I made it over to the window and sure enough there was this dark sports-utility vehicle everyone drives nowadays, blocking Phil's car."

"Did you see anything else?" Griff asked.

"Well, I heard a slam—I think it was the vehicle thingy's back door or trunk." She stopped. "Do those things have trunks?" She waved the question off. "Anyway. I did make out two big, black shadows racing to the driver and passenger doors and then speeding off. This time when they ran over the garbage can, they dragged it out to the middle of the street. Unfortunately, that's going to be another fine for poor Philip." She shook her head. "Rules are rules."

Without looking at each other, Kyson and Griffin shook their heads in commiseration for the people who had the misfortune to live under this board's charge.

"Did you get a look at these, uh, big, black shadows?" Kyson asked in his best Joe Friday voice.

"Unfortunately, no," Juanita said, looking disappointed. "Everything happened so fast, I forgot to grab my infrared binoculars."

"Or call the hotline for backup," Louise added in equal disappointment. "Really. What's the point in investing in all this if we're not going to use them or follow the set guidelines?"

The other women mumbled their agreement.

Juanita appeared thoroughly chastised.

"You have infrared binoculars?" Kyson asked, astonished.

"It allows us to be able to see in the dark," Juanita perked. "Most crimes happen in the middle of the night, so it seemed like a great investment," she answered as if it all made perfect sense.

"And you each have a pair?" Griff asked the group.

Again, they performed another round of head bobbing.

"And yet, you didn't see anything last night?"

"Well, I went to bed early because I had a dreadful headache." Juanita swallowed. "I didn't follow protocol last night. I swear it's the first time I, uh, sort of fell asleep on the job."

Kyson couldn't help but ask, "Is there a fine for that?"

Juanita's mouth flattened.

"Just asking," he said and tried to backpedal his way onto her good side by returning to the subject at hand. "What did you do next?"

"Well, nothing," she admitted. "It may be a violation to leave your garbage can in the middle of the street, but it's certainly not against the law," she reasoned. "It wasn't until this morning when I walked over to deliver the violation ticket that I got a chance to talk to Phil's sweet new girlfriend. Sweet woman," she stopped to add. "He must have been hiding her under lock and key. I've never seen her around before. She said when she came over she found the place ransacked and that's when I *knew*," she said.

The pause was deliberate, so Kyson decided to play along. "You knew what?"

"That *she* was behind it."

Kyson ignored the woman's tone.

"By *she,* do you mean Mr. Matthews's ex-wife?" Griff asked.

"Absolutely," Juanita insisted while the gray-and-white-haired ladies surrounding her nodded. "If there's foul play to be had in this neighborhood, you better bet the farm that Michael woman is the root of it."

Chapter 6

Peyton loved her life.

She had a wonderful husband, great family, successful career, nice home and now she was looking forward to motherhood. But she was totally over her future bundle of joy sitting on top of her bladder.

"Uh-oh." Her husband, Lincoln, lowered his Sudoku puzzle book. "I know that look. You're having one of your strange cravings," he assessed and then climbed to his feet. "What would you like? Peanut butter and pickle sandwich or ice cream and pickles?"

"No. That's not it." She struggled to stand.

Lincoln zoomed to her side and helped her up. "Bathroom?"

Peyton nodded. "Bathroom." At her look of misery, Lincoln gave her a peck on the nose.

"How about I make a sandwich for you anyway?"

She wobbled her way toward the hall. "Make it the ice cream and pickles and you got yourself a deal."

"I'm headed to the kitchen now."

Her trip to the bathroom felt like a twenty-minute cardiovascular workout, and on her way back to the living room, the pain in her back made her wish for an early delivery.

Bam! Bam! Bam!

Peyton jumped, mainly because she was walking by the door when the abrupt series of hard knocks hammered the wood. "Gee whiz. Is there a fire?" she mumbled.

"Who's at the door?" Lincoln called out from the kitchen.

"I don't know," she said and inquired through the door, "Who is it?"

"It's us!"

Peyton rolled her eyes. She didn't know exactly which grouping of the family members qualified as "us," but she had hoped to have a private day vegging out on the sofa with her husband. The last thing she wanted was any of the normal shenanigans that were associated with her sisters.

"It's just the girls," Peyton yelled to her husband.

"If you get rid of them, there may be a foot massage in it for you," he promised as he passed the hallway, waving her bowl of ice cream and jar of dill pickles.

"Say no more," she responded and opened the door. She took one look at the Nosy Sisters Network and told them to, "Go away," and then promptly slammed the door in their faces.

Michael blinked, closed her mouth and then glanced at her sisters. "What the hell?"

Sheldon crossed her arms and muttered, "Heck, I don't blame her."

Frankie's grunt sounded like agreement.

Michael faced the door again, determined to bang the damn thing down if need be. This time when the door opened, Lincoln's tall frame filled the threshold.

"Can I help you ladies?"

Michael swallowed. Linc was quite a formidable figure. It seemed completely laughable that three years ago she believed him to be her brother's boyfriend instead of her sister's.

Frankie stepped forward. "Can Peyton come out and play?"

"Well, to tell you the truth, girls, we sort of wanted to spend the day together," he said with an apologetic smile. But when three sets of eyes only blinked up at him, he added, "Alone. We wanted to spend time together alone."

No response.

"So if you want to maybe—I don't know—come back tomorrow?"

Again—silence.

Finally, he heaved a deep breath. He knew his sisters-in-law well enough to know their wall of silence meant they weren't leaving until they got what they wanted. "Fine. I'll go get her. But you only get five minutes, girls. I mean it." Without waiting for their agreement, Lincoln disappeared back into the house.

A few seconds later, an irritated Peyton returned to the door. "I told you all to go away."

Michael and Frankie each grabbed one of Peyton's arms and dragged her out through the front door.

"What on earth?"

Sheldon closed the door and quickly followed behind the girls down the walkway.

"We got ourselves in a bit of a situation," Michael said.

"We?" Sheldon and Frankie echoed in unison when they came to a stop behind Michael's black Volvo.

"Yes—we!" Mike insisted, digging out her car keys from her pants pocket. "We're all in this together now." She jabbed the key into the trunk.

"How come I get the feeling I don't want to know what you guys are talking about?" Peyton asked, glancing around.

Michael popped open the trunk.

Peyton looked down and screamed.

Three hands clamped around Peyton's mouth while Phil, hog-tied and gagged, squirmed and bucked in the trunk.

"Keep it down," Michael hissed. "The last thing we need is to draw attention."

Peyton's hands clamped around her bulging belly.

"Just great!" Sheldon panicked. "We're going to send her into early labor. I told you, Mikey, this was a bad idea."

"Calm down," Michael coached her baby sister. "Take a deep breath."

Peyton followed the instructions and her sisters peeled their hands away in order for her to exhale. However, she didn't stop clutching her belly or backing away from the car.

"I know this looks bad," Michael said gently. Somehow she reasoned if she talked low and soft she could keep the panic to a reasonable level.

"Have you all gone crazy?"

"I'm going to vote yes," Frankie said.

"Same here," Sheldon added.

Phil mumbled something that also sounded like it was in the affirmative.

"Please tell me you guys are playing some kind of game," Peyton begged. "If so, I don't want any part of it."

Michael didn't want any part of it, either. In fact, she still held out a thread of hope all of this was part of some crazy dream. Maybe someone slipped something into one of her drinks last night and this was just a nightmare with apparently no end in sight.

"Look, P.J.," Mike said, stepping forward. "Please say you still have Ricky's number—or some way to contact him."

"Ricky?" Peyton asked. "Ricky who?"

"Your ex-husband, Ricky," Sheldon said. "Wasn't he best friends with the Damon twins?"

Peyton grunted and rolled her eyes. "You mean the *Demon* twins, don't you?"

Sheldon glanced at Mikey, smirking. "I told you so."

"Granted, their methods are a little extreme, but up until last night I've always viewed them as harmless," Michael confessed.

"Wait. Ray and Scott are behind this?" Peyton asked. "Okay. I *definitely* don't want anything to do with whatever the heck is going on." Peyton turned. "I'm going back into my crime-free house and I'm going to pretend you guys were never here."

The three sisters blocked Peyton's escape.

"You can't just act like you didn't see anything. Phil is threatening to throw us in jail for kidnapping."

"I'd say he has a pretty good case."

"And what—you think he's going to omit you refused to help him?"

"Fine. I'll call the police."

Michael easily called her bluff. "You'll do no such

thing. Besides, the police have already been to my place this morning, asking about his disappearance."

"What?" Peyton clutched her belly again. "Mike, this is serious!"

"What? You think I don't know that?" Michael snapped. Her patience was at an end and her blood pressure was at an all-time high. "I'm trying to find those damn twins so they can convince my idiot of an ex-husband I did *not* instruct them to kidnap him, or at the very least tell him I was plastered and didn't mean any of it."

"Why don't you just tell him that yourself?"

"He doesn't believe me!"

Sheldon and Frankie coughed.

"No one believes me!" Michael amended. Her eyes burned with a sudden rush of tears. What the hell? Maybe she should just cut Phil loose and then just take her chances trying to convince a jury. Yet, at the same time, if she couldn't convince her family, she stood no chance of convincing a jury of her peers.

Peyton drew a deep breath—several, actually— while she clearly weighed her options.

"Please, P.J." Michael dropped to her knees, her hands forming a steeple. "If you do this for me, I swear I'll never ask you to do another thing."

Her baby sister's brows lifted in obvious disbelief.

"Hell," Frankie said, jabbing a fist into her hip. "What about us?"

Michael ignored them, but kept her pleading gaze on Peyton.

"Oh, all right," Peyton gave in. "Who knows, maybe we'll all get to share a room in the mental ward."

Michael caught a movement from the corner of her eye and turned to see that Phil had managed to sit up in the trunk. "Oh, no you don't." She climbed back onto her feet, pushed him down and closed the trunk. When she faced her sisters again, they were all just staring and shaking their heads.

"Oh, he'll be fine. Let's just hurry and find that number. The faster we find the twins, the faster we can end this nightmare."

Peyton turned and led the way back to the house. Michael followed while Frankie and Sheldon brought up the rear.

"I just thought of something," Frankie whispered to Sheldon.

"What's that?"

"Can you ever remember a time when Michael's plans worked out?"

Sheldon fell silent, thinking.

"Yeah," Frankie said. "Me neither."

By the time Kyson and his partner returned to the station, their notepads were full and their heads were spinning with information regarding the ex-Mrs. Matthews. Kyson had no doubt that the geriatric Neighborhood Watch gang would've held them hostage longer if Griff hadn't faked a call from the captain and then lied about having to return to the station.

"There's only so much mothballs and Ben-Gay a man can take," Griff said.

Kyson agreed. Now that he was back at his desk, he immediately pecked Michael's name into the police files, hoping the elderly women had exaggerated their former neighbor's character.

They hadn't.

"Oh my God, take a look at this," he said, staring at the screen.

Griff stood from his desk and rushed around to Kyson's.

On-screen, the computer looked as if it was going haywire as arrests, citations, warnings and detailed footnotes scrolled before them.

"I told you she was an odd bird, didn't I?" Griff leaned forward, reading what was being printed on-screen. "It doesn't look like she was booked for anything too serious." He chortled. "Looks like she's one hell of a prankster."

Kyson released a low whistle. "That, or she has anger-management issues."

Scrolling with the mouse, the partners quickly learned that all charges in Michael Adams's criminal file were eventually dropped.

"Either the woman is incredibly lucky or most people are afraid to cross her," Kyson concluded.

"I'm going to place my money on the latter," Griff said, straightening and then shuffling his way back over to his desk. "Hopefully her file has softened that hard-on you have for the chick." He plopped down in his seat. "Those old ladies were on to your girl."

Kyson ignored the comment and stared at Michael's arrest pictures. Even looking at those was a source of amusement. The woman had put an artistic spin on posing with her arrest numbers as if she'd been hired for comedy stills. There were pictures of her throwing deuces, sticking her tongue out, flipping a bird and even a few of her blowing kisses.

"Oh, God," Griff moaned. "You still have it bad for her, don't you?"

Again, Kyson didn't answer, but pulled out his notepad and began typing in this morning's notes.

Griff laughed and shook his head. "All right. Don't say I didn't warn you when we have to smack the handcuffs on her over this whole mess."

"What? You really think she had something to do with her husband's disappearance?"

"And you don't?"

Did he? Kyson didn't want to admit he'd pretty much turned off his policeman's intuition the moment this voluptuous goddess opened the door. Hell, he hadn't been *this* affected by a woman since…since…Jada.

"Never mind," Griff said, studying his partner. "I got my answer."

"I think we're jumping ahead of ourselves," Kyson finally said. "Philip Matthews has only been missing for a few hours. So his house was a little wrecked. The man could be a lousy housekeeper for all we know."

"Sort of like his ex-wife?"

"She just moved in."

Griff shook his head. "You got it bad."

"I'm just stating the facts. There's no proof any crime has been committed. Just a report from a concerned girlfriend of Matthews's, who no one knew about. Who knows, maybe he had more than one drink and decided to take off and celebrate his freedom papers? Heck, *she* threw a party."

Griff shrugged as if he could buy that excuse. "Time will tell. But..." He paused and then shook his head. "Never mind."

His partner's hesitancy piqued Kyson's curiosity. "What is it?"

Griff paused a little longer before saying, "Well, it's just that after meeting Ms. Adams, hearing about her misadventures in her former neighborhood *and* seeing her mile-long rap sheet, she doesn't strike me as the sort to be afraid of anything."

"Me neither," Kyson said. "What's your point?"

"No point," Griff confessed. "I just wonder what the chances are that she's really afraid of rats. And if not—"

"Then what spooked her in the basement?" Kyson finished his partner's sentence.

"Not just her, but her sister Sheldon, as well."

Chapter 7

Michael had never prayed so hard and so many times in one day in her life. And no matter how hard she tried to maintain her hard-as-nails persona for her sisters, she was sure they could now see the visible cracks. How could they not? Her ex-husband was tied and gagged in the trunk of her car, for Pete's sake.

Maybe it's time to admit that I've finally cracked?

She couldn't remember when she'd started with her tough-girl routine. Maybe being the middle child, she figured she needed to do something in order to stand out in a family of six children. Sheldon didn't have to do anything for entitlement.

She was the oldest. Of course, she was known for having a buttload of children.

Frankie was the first to marry a multimillionaire and she rarely missed an opportunity to rub that into people's faces. Joey was the second—marrying a well-to-do director and now shooting her very own movie. Peyton, the baby girl in the family, was successful in her own right—a big-time art agent who was now married to a man who was blazing a trail with his own artwork.

And what did she have?

She was divorced from a man who took years to get to the altar. No career. No children. She was just a plus-size woman knocking on forty with no clue on how to start her life all over—depending on whether she would have a life that didn't include prison bars when this was all over.

"It's gotta be in here somewhere," Peyton said, rummaging through another chest of drawers in her bedroom. Each of her sisters was assigned to different boxes or closets, looking for Peyton's old pink datebook.

"I always thought you were a little more organized than this," Sheldon complained, closing the door to the armoire.

"I wasn't exactly trying to keep up with Ricky after the divorce. Since I haven't heard of him blowing up the music world, I'd just assumed that he'd found some other sugar momma to take care of his grown butt."

"Someone is still bitter," Frankie commented.

"Hardly," Peyton countered. "I've definitely upgraded."

Michael had to agree. The fact that Peyton had found true love the second time around gave Michael hope, however small.

A deep rumble by the bedroom door caused the women to jump, but when they all turned to see Peyton's husband filling the doorway, everyone visibly relaxed.

"Mind if I ask what you girls are doing?" he asked.

No one said anything, including his wife.

"How about a hint?" he asked.

Silence.

A twitch of annoyance flashed along his jaw-line, but he obviously figured out no one was going to answer his question and he finally turned away from the door.

"All right then," he acquiesced. "I'll leave you girls to your secrets."

Once his footsteps disappeared down the hall-way, Peyton turned to Michael with her eyes blazing. "This better not come back to bite me on the ass," she warned. "I'll never forgive you if I'm dragged to jail and forced to give birth behind bars."

Michael drew a ragged breath and then lowered her gaze back to the pile of books and memorabilia.

What could she say? What did everyone expect her to say?

"Look, girls. Let's just stop." She slammed the drawer closed. "I'm sorry I've dragged you all into this. This is my problem and I should be the one to face the music. Maybe I did tell Ray and Scotty to do what they did. I don't know. I don't remember." Michael walked over to Peyton's king-size bed and plopped down. "I really messed up this time." She hung her head just as tears crested her eyelids and slid down her face.

It didn't go unnoticed by Michael that her sisters were a bit slow in drifting over to surround and support her. She could hardly blame them. In all Michael's years of outrageous stunts and petty vengeful tactics, her actions rarely affected just her.

She was thirty-eight and it was time to grow up.

Sheldon was the first to sit next to her and loop a supportive arm around her shoulders. "No matter what happens, we're going to be there for you."

Peyton, with her bulging belly, sat on her right side and did the same thing. "Of course we will. Just not in the cell with you."

Frankie leaned against the closet door and folded her arms. "Amen."

Despite her misery, her sisters' grudging support drew a smile from Michael. "I guess I can't ask for any more than that."

"Um, excuse me," Linc's heavy baritone sliced

through the mini pity party. "Whatever you girls are in here whispering about doesn't have anything to do with Phil popping out of Michael's trunk like a jack-in-a-box, does it?"

"What?" the girls thundered as they jumped to attention.

Linc stepped back as if afraid he was about to be attacked by his crazed group of sisters-in-law. "Yeah, I just saw him hop out of the trunk and take off running down the driveway."

This time Linc did jump out of the way as Michael, Sheldon, Frankie and his wobbling wife rushed out the bedroom and out of the house.

A million thoughts raced through Michael's head as she led the pack outside, but the moment she saw her car's trunk propped open, she knew it was all over. Still, she ran all the way to the car and glanced inside the now-empty compartment.

"Somebody just shoot me."

As usual, at the end of his shift, Kyson drove to his neighborhood gym and proceeded to work out his stress and frustrations by punching a hundred-eighty-pound bag until he was drenched in sweat. Today, he had plenty to work off.

Nine years on the force, eighteen months of those in homicide, and it still wasn't any easier knowing that each day he went to work he had to deal with senseless murders, ruthless drug dealers and combustible marriages. And nearly everyone he had to talk to, investigate or interrogate hated the police.

It was a thankless job.

Only a few understood why he did it: Jada. He sighed and pulled his thoughts from that minefield and returned to punching the bag.

Minutes later, Kyson stopped long enough to pace and catch his breath.

"You know, if I didn't know any better, I'd say that punching bag owed you money."

Kyson's head turned at the familiar purr and he leveled a smile at the gym's owner and resident hard body, Crystal King. "Well, look who blew back into town."

"Missed me much?" She smiled and approached him with her arms flung open wide.

Kyson accepted the hug but couldn't stop chuckling when Crystal hung on a little too long and used the time to feel him up. "C'mon now. Don't make me slam the cuffs on you."

"Promise?"

He laughed. "Women like you are how fools like me end up in a chalk outline. Where's your husband?"

She finally stepped back. "Oh, he's around here somewhere." She shrugged. "He's probably peeking in on the strip classes upstairs."

Laughing, Kyson turned back to the punching bag. He didn't have time for the type of games Crystal played. She spent most of her time flirting and propositioning her gym members in hopes of remedying her husband's attention-deficit problem.

"How come you don't have a woman?" she asked after watching him take a few jabs. "A six-four, dark-chocolate brother like you should have women dripping off of him."

"I am married," he said, bouncing on the balls of his feet.

"What—to your job?"

"What I do is important."

"Whatever." She laughed. "A fine specimen like you should be settled down with a woman and making chocolate babies."

He stopped punching as his laughter deepened. "Where are *your* babies?"

"Are you kidding? My husband is pumped up on steroids. Half the time he can't get it up, let alone get me pregnant."

"Sounds like the makings of a happy marriage."

"Hmmph!"

He eyeballed her. "If you're so unhappy, why don't you just divorce him?"

Crystal shrugged as her expression pinched. "Because I love the idiot—even if he is shooting blanks."

"So you're in it to win it?"

"You got it. And if he ever even thought about leaving *me*—I'd kill him."

Kyson shook his head. "You might want to rethink telling a cop that."

"Please," Crystal said, following him to his water bottle and towel. "No body. No crime. Everyone knows that."

Kyson stopped in his tracks. "What did you say?"

Chapter 8

Luscious mounds of pecan-brown skin pressed against Kyson's hard chest. A light, feathery moan filled his head while he concentrated on rotating his hips just right. Each stroke elevated his heart rate. Soon he would either explode with an unbelievable orgasm or die from a massive heart attack. Gazing into Michael's rapturous face made either prognosis worth the risk.

Thick, strong thighs wrapped around his waist and anchored Kyson in place, allowing him to sink deeper into his dream lover's warm honeypot.

This was heaven.

Through the mesh of his dark eyelashes, he

watched as Michael pressed her large breasts together. Twin raisin-size nipples surrounded by a pair of beautiful caramel areolae hypnotized him as they bounced and jiggled before his eyes. His mouth watered while unbelievable hunger pains forced him to bury his head in the deep valley between her breasts. He feasted like a starved man—greedy for every inch of her sweet body.

At the feel of her vaginal muscles tightening and milking his essence, he instinctively knew she was on the brink of an orgasm.

"That's it, baby," he coached. "That's it. Give it to me."

Give it to him, she did.

His own control slipped, an amazing sensation unfolded, rendering his ability to breathe almost impossible. "I'm coming, baby," he warned, already feeling the pending explosion.

Michael opened her eyes, locked gazes with him in order to deepen their bond at this crucial time.

If it was timed just right, they could come together. Judging by her own choppy breathing, it was going to happen in the next four, three, two, one—

Riinnng! Riinng!

Kyson's eyes flew open at the sound of his alarm clock. He shot up in bed, glanced around, disoriented. When he recognized his small bedroom and noticed the empty space next to him, disappointment stabbed him so deep, it felt like a real physical wound.

For a few long seconds, he allowed the alarm clock to ring while he sank his head into the palms of his hands. When he finally shut it off, a part of him still couldn't believe what he'd experienced was just a dream.

It felt so real.

Kyson pulled back the bed's top sheet and climbed out. This morning's hard-on was harder and throbbed mercilessly and threatened his no-sex-or-masturbation-during-training rule.

For years, Kyson had been an ultimate fighting fan—a style of mixed martial arts competition. Throughout his life he'd studied jujitsu, judo, karate, kickboxing, tae kwon do and wrestling, but he'd never given thought to become a fighter.

The suggestion came from his older brother, Khail, a onetime UFC titleholder himself. An unfortunate knee injury had ended Khail's career, but he never wasted an opportunity to fill Kyson's head with similar hopes and dreams.

The truth of the matter was that Kyson wasn't so sure a UFC title was what he really wanted. He just loved how the intense training and fighting relieved much of his job's stresses.

Kyson, as he'd done for the past three days, recalled his visit to Michael Adams's home. Remembered in vivid detail how his body had ignored years of training and responded to the curvy beauty like he was a hormone-driven teenager.

Despite a shower the night before, Kyson hit the shower again that morning, using more than a generous amount of baby oil when he closed his eyes and replayed his vivid dream frame by frame.

Brown skin.

Hard, dark nipples.

Soft, thick thighs.

Warm, slick honeypot…

Toes curled and weak-kneed, Kyson threw back his head as his climactic groan bounced and echoed off the tiles around him. For several seconds afterward, his ears hummed while blood rushed from his head.

"Kyson!"

Catching his name above the steady stream of water, Kyson shut it off.

"Kyson!"

"Khail," he mumbled and pulled open the shower door. "Just a second!" He grabbed a navy-colored towel and wrapped it around his hips.

As usual, he discovered his brother bent over headlong into the refrigerator. "Why don't you ever eat at your place?" he asked. "You know how small a brother's paycheck is on the force."

Khail stood with an armful of food. "And it's my fault you didn't take a job utilizing your engineering degree because…?"

"The point is, I'm on a budget," Kyson said, an

expert at dodging his brother's loaded questions. "Missed you at the gym—again."

"Sorry. It's was my and Aimee's six-months-since-we-met anniversary last night. Had to do it up for her."

"Wasn't it yours and Brenda's anniversary last week?"

"Yeah. I need to start meeting chicks in different months, for real."

"You're supposed to be my trainer, remember?"

"I know. I know." Khail nodded, making himself at home while he prepared himself a monster sandwich. "You better hurry and get dressed if you're going to get your four-mile run in before you head off to work."

"I'm off today."

"What? They finally give a brother a day off?"

"Yeah, but my partner's not so lucky. He's training a rookie today."

The phone rang.

"The department," the brothers grumbled in unison.

Kyson answered the call by the third ring and was pleasantly surprised to discover it wasn't the department, but his baby sister, Naomi.

"'Happy birthday to you,'" she launched into the verse the moment he answered. She performed the whole song groggy and off-key, but that was what made it all the more adorable. Plus, she was making the long-distance call from Georgia, which made it even more special.

"Thanks, Baby G." Kyson looked over his shoulder at his brother, who was just taking his first bite of his sandwich. "I'm glad *someone* remembered what day it was."

Khail stopped chewing and then started speaking with a mouthful of food. "Oh, snap. It's your birthday, huh?"

Kyson rolled his eyes and returned his attention to his sister. "Thanks for calling, Baby G. When you coming out this way again?"

"When the ground stops shaking and those damn trees stop burning." She laughed. "I keep trying to tell you and Khail that California is going to drop off into the ocean. But a hard head will make a soft butt."

Kyson laughed. "Then I guess that means I'm going to have to trek back to the Dirty South if I'm going to see my favorite sister in the whole world."

"Funny. I'm your only sister."

"Good thing," he volleyed. "The world wouldn't have been able to take two of you."

Kyson, the middle child of the three siblings, was generally considered the levelheaded one. He was oftentimes odd man out among his friends for actually believing the legal system could work. He had to believe in order to make sense out of being a cop.

A damn good cop.

"So, are you keeping to your rule on your birthday?" Naomi probed.

"What?"

"You know. No sex until fight night."

Kyson chuckled. "You have your nose too far up my business, little girl."

"Hell, I just want you to get a life." She snickered and then yawned. "It's a damn shame your baby sister gets more than you these days."

"With who?" he thundered protectively. "What's his name? What does he do? Who are his people?"

Naomi just laughed. "Chill. You're crazy if you think I'm about to tell you or knuckleheaded Khail my business so you can run police and credit checks on them. I can handle my own business."

Kyson was silent, wondering if he should call up some of his old high-school boys in Atlanta and put a tag on Naomi. She didn't know men like he knew them, and the last thing he wanted was to see her hurt. "All right. I'm gonna leave it alone."

"Good."

"For now," he amended.

"Whatever. You just make sure you find yourself a nice birthday present," she teased. "Breaking your no-sex rule this *one* time won't be the end of the world."

"I'm hanging up," he said, determined not to have this conversation.

"All right. I'm just trying to help out."

"Thanks, but I think I can handle my own sex life." Despite that it currently consisted of him whacking off in the shower.

The moment he ended the call, Khail wrapped an arm around his neck and held him in a choke hold.

"Happy birthday, little man." Khail rubbed his knuckles against the top of Kyson's head and then released him shortly before he passed out. "Tell you what. No training today. It's officially your day off."

"I take it this means you didn't buy a gift?"

"I'm going to get you something better than a gift," Khail boasted. "I'm going to get you laid. It's been a few months since you broke up with that psycho you were dating. It's time to get your feet wet again."

"That's all right," Kyson said, remembering the near-anorexic women with fake double D's Khail usually dated. "I can handle my own love life."

"Love?" Khail said, truly perplexed. "Who said anything about love? This is about getting laid so you can stop jerking off in the shower."

For three days Michael waited on pins and needles for the police to return and haul her off to jail. Three days of eating everything that wasn't nailed down. Three days of packing her clothes and then unpacking them at the thought of living the rest of her life on the run.

For the first time in her life, Michael was completely at someone else's mercy. The thought of it being her ex-husband made it all the worse.

Of course, her nerves might have been a little better if her sisters would stop calling every other hour. Then again, they had every reason to be as anxious as she did. Phil had threatened to have them all thrown in jail.

This stalling tactic either meant Phil had had a change of heart or he'd learned a few tricks of her trade and was making her and her sisters sweat. If it was the latter, she was impressed.

The phone rang.

Michael jumped. When she realized it was just a telephone, she nearly fainted with relief, but then remembered that bad news often came by phone. Crossing her bedroom, she looked at the caller-ID console on the nightstand. This time, she allowed herself to collapse on the bed, relieved to see Joey's cell number.

"Hey, Joey. What's up?"

"You're kidding, right?" Joey laughed. "Don't tell me you forgot about tonight."

"Tonight?"

Joey sighed and then laughed. "So you did forget. Figures. Let me guess, you're still playing Nancy Drew with your ex. Girl, exhale already before you do something you'll regret. You're getting too old for us to keep bailing you out of jail."

If she only knew. So far, Joey was the only sister

who didn't know about Phil's kidnapping and escape. So far, she and her other sisters saw no reason to drag Joey into it. They were pretty much just hoping Phil had calmed down and chalked the episode up as another one of Michael's wild pranks.

Keyword was *hoping*.

"Michael, are you still there?"

"Yeah, I'm still here. Changing the subject, what did I forget about tonight?"

"Dad and Donna's first anniversary."

Michael groaned. Only the shenanigans of the past few days could have made her forget about their father's anniversary party. While it was still strange to have another sister—one that was thirty-six years younger—she found it even harder to accept her new stepmother.

They all had.

"Yeah. Yeah. It's all starting to come back to me now."

"Don't worry about it. I hear the mind is the first thing to go."

Michael rolled her eyes. "Laugh all you want. You're just a year behind me."

"A year and a half," Joey corrected. "Get it right."

Michael appreciated and welcomed this short reprieve and laughed. But going out tonight, when she was still waiting for Phil to make his intentions clear made her more than a little wary about going out. "Look, Joey, about tonight—"

"Don't even think about canceling. If I have to go, then so do you."

Silence.

"Mikey," Joey insisted. "We promised Dad we would put more of an effort into welcoming Donna into the family."

"I know. I know," Michael huffed. The main problem the Adams clan had with the whole Donna issue was the *way* their father had kept his relationship with this mysterious *young* woman hush-hush. That is, until he knocked her up and then did the gentlemanly thing by marrying her.

For years he'd hid his playboy ways under the ruse of poker night out with the boys. Actually, it was a stroke of genius to keep his nosy daughters out of his personal life. However, the end result was his six older children having a stranger as a new stepmother and a new sister: Theodore Jamal Adams—Teddy for short.

In a nutshell, their father's marriage was awkward for everyone involved.

"I'll go," Michael said, deflated.

"All right. Knew we could count on you, Mikey," Joey bubbled.

"I'll see you in a little while," Mike said.

"Good. Don't be late."

Michael's smile disappeared the moment she ended the call. She did not want to do this. After a quick shower, Michael painted on her best face, squeezed into a pair of jeans that she refused to admit were too small and tossed on a low-cut tee that showed off her bodacious tah-tahs.

"Enjoy freedom while you can," she said to her reflection and left the house. Still, when she climbed into the car and pulled out of the driveway, she couldn't shake the feeling that someone was watching her.

From across the street, the tip of a cigarette glowed orange while the driver behind the wheel of a black Ford Explorer watched as Michael Adams pulled out of her driveway and drove off just as the evening made its transition to night.

"Don't lose her," the woman in the passenger seat said.

"I won't," the driver responded, starting the car.

Chapter 9

Marlin and Donna's one-year anniversary looked and felt more like a wake. Cloistered together in the back of Nicolino's, the Adams clan made an awkward attempt to smile and be merry. The constant absence of Donna's family members remained a source of curiosity.

Surely the woman had some family tucked away somewhere?

But Michael's keen investigative skills turned up nothing. It was like the woman had just appeared out of thin air. Shortly before her father's marriage, Michael had tried to talk to him about Donna's mysterious past. He'd exploded and made it clear he wanted her to butt out of his private affairs.

Reluctantly, she complied…for now.

The other elephant in the room was the fact that Teddy looked nothing like Marlin or really even her mother. When Teddy was born, no one said anything about the baby's pale coloring.

All babies were pale when they were born.

Well, it was nearly one year later and the Adamses were still waiting for the baby's coloring to fill in and for her eyes to turn from a smoky-gray to brown.

Still, Teddy was an adorable child. Sweet-tempered and playful, the newest Adams also seemed to really take to Michael. In turn, Michael fell hard for Teddy.

"Gift time," Sheldon exclaimed.

"Gifts?" Michael repeated. "You all brought gifts?" She glanced around and sure enough, her sisters started pulling out beautifully wrapped boxes with shiny bows. How come no one told her they were bringing gifts?

Frankie came to her rescue. "Here." She slid over a card. "Sign your name and we'll tell them this one is from both of us."

"Thanks." Michael jotted her name on the card. Of course people brought gifts to an anniversary party, she scolded herself. What was the matter with her? Was her A-game that severely off?

"Buon compleanno! Buon compleanno!"

Michael turned at the sound of a group of people singing. Toward the restaurant's bar, a group of waiters and waitresses surrounded a table.

"It must be someone's birthday," Joey commented.

Michael nodded and returned her attention to Teddy, who was busy coloring in the restaurant's coloring book for children.

"Hey, isn't that the cop who was at your place the other day?" Sheldon whispered.

Michael's and Frankie's heads whipped around.

"What cop?" P.J. and Joey asked.

"You know, it does look like him."

"What cop?" Joey asked again.

"You mean the one that…?" P.J.'s question trailed into nothing.

Michael didn't say anything. She couldn't. The moment her gaze landed on Detective Dekker's smooth, dark-chocolate skin, her body started acting as if it was trying to combat a fever. She felt light-headed, and her heart raced at the mere sight of him.

"What *cop?*" Joey insisted.

"It *is* him," Sheldon and Frankie agreed simultaneously.

"Um." Michael pushed her chair back and forced herself to stand. "I'll be right back."

"Mike, what are you going to do?" Sheldon asked, alarmed.

"Nothing," she said. "I'm just going over to wish him a happy birthday."

"Why?" Frankie asked. "Leave well enough alone."

"I agree," P.J. emphasized.

"Okay. One of you need to tell me what the heck is going on." Joey set her fork down and crossed her arms.

"Give it up," Linc said, leaning over in a conspiratorial whisper. "They just blink and stare at me whenever I ask a question, too."

"You guys keep secrets from me?" Hurt pinched Joey's expression.

"Trust me," P.J. said, rubbing her belly. "You don't want to know this one."

"Guys, I'll be right back," Michael insisted, and then moved away from the table before anyone could stop her, which was probably the right thing to do under the circumstances.

What *was* she doing? Playing with fire?

As she crossed the restaurant, Michael hand pressed her clothes down, patted her hair, hoping it still looked good, and licked her lips for a natural gloss.

Would he remember her? Did she want him to? Just thinking about the hideous plaid and polka-dot pajama ensemble she'd worn the last time she saw him should've had her running in the opposite direction instead of gravitating toward the man.

The singing waiters and waitresses parted and Detective Fine's dark eyes landed on her during her final approach. If she wasn't mistaken, a faint smile softened the corners of his lips as recognition settled in.

"Ms. Adams," he greeted, standing.

She smiled. "Ah, so you do remember me?"

"What can I say?" His eyes roamed over her figure. "You leave quite an impression."

Michael braced her hands on the back of an empty chair. Just being around him had a strange effect on her nervous system.

"Hmmph. Hmmph."

Michael glanced to her left and for the first time noticed the other handsome man sitting at the table.

"Ms. Adams—"

"Michael," she corrected him. "You're off the clock, right?"

A wide smile monopolized his broad face. "Right. Michael, I'd like for you to meet my older brother, Khail. Khail, Michael."

Khail joined his brother standing. "An interesting name for a beautiful woman."

"A strong name for a strong woman," Michael countered, teasing. "It's a pleasure to meet you," she added, noting the strong resemblance between the two men. However, no sparks or electricity coursed between them when he took her hand nor when he lifted it to his mouth for a brief kiss.

"Trust me," Khail said. "The pleasure is all mine."

Michael felt the slight caress against her palm

and her eyebrows rose high at the man's subtle way of making his interest known. She batted her eyes, but pulled her hand from his grip in silent rejection.

When her eyes drifted back to the man who'd captured her attention, she was stunned to see his open friendliness had cooled considerably. Was he jealous?

The thought tickled and flattered her. Apparently divorce didn't mean she was out of the game for good.

"Anyway," she said, turning the charm on to full blast, "I just came over to say hi to the birthday boy."

"Nonsense," Khail said. "You should join us."

"Can't," she said with obvious regret. "My family is celebrating my father's first anniversary."

"You've been celebrating quite a bit this week," Kyson said.

"Don't worry. This time, I plan to stay away from the alcohol," she joked.

"Glad to hear it."

Despite running out of things to say, Michael remained rooted behind the chair and allowed an awkward silence to drift over the trio for a solid minute. Actually, if Khail hadn't suddenly interrupted into a coughing fit, she was sure that she and Kyson would have been content to just stare and mentally remove each other's clothes.

"Well, I guess I'd better get back to my party," Michael said, hoping the logic would get her legs to uproot themselves.

"It was great seeing you again…Michael."

"Enjoy the rest of your birthday," she said, and then for some unexplainable, *crazy* reason, she moved from behind the safety of her chair to stand by the handsome detective.

A stunned Kyson had just spent the last two minutes trying to keep his eyes from dipping down and staring at the voluptuous goddess's full breasts. Now he couldn't have stopped watching their approach if his badge had depended on it.

Then they were lifting toward him as Michael leaned up on her toes, but there was nothing to compare the sensation he felt when her breasts pressed into his chest a second before her pillow-soft lips landed against his cheek.

"Happy birthday," she murmured.

When her warm breath drifted across his ear, his hard-on pressed back in response and embarrassed him.

Michael glanced down and then turned her sparkling gaze back up at him. She didn't say anything, but then again, she didn't have to with that wide Cheshire grin she gave before slinking away.

"Well, I'll be damned," Khail said in the wake of her swinging hips. "Now *that's* what I call a woman!"

Kyson slid back down into his chair, his body still erect and ready.

"How did you meet that brick house and what's with all the covert rubbing up on you? Are you tapping that and keeping secrets?" Khail asked and returned to his seat.

Kyson frowned. "Down, boy. Down."

"Just answer the question. Are you into her? And if not, can I get the digits?" He twirled around in his seat to see whether he could still see her. "Damn, bro. I think I'm in love."

"You always think you're in love."

Khail tossed a smile over his shoulder. "You know me so well." He turned back around in his seat and leveled a stern look at Kyson. "You, on the other hand, never let a woman ruffle your feathers. And you certainly looked ruffled right now."

If only you knew. Kyson reached for his sweet iced tea, and wished like hell it was something a little stronger to take the edge off his erection. Damn. He could still feel the impression of her nipples against his chest and smell the Chanel No. 5.

"You don't know what you're talking about."

"Please." Khail laughed as he resumed eating his meal. "There were enough pheromones between you guys to set off an orgy up in this place. Now answer the question—are you feeling homegirl or not?"

Backed into a corner, Kyson cast a glance toward the back of the restaurant just as Michael looked up. In an instant, their eyes locked.

"Oh, yeah." Khail laughed again. "You're definitely feeling homegirl."

* * *

Michael stayed three hours instead of the one she'd promised herself. The main reason may have had something to do with the fact she didn't want to stop gazing at Detective Dekker. But what she saw, she certainly didn't like. Minutes after returning to her seat, two women joined the Dekker brothers at their table.

Actually, calling them women was being kind. They were more like anorexic hoochies with twin bowling balls for breasts. How they were able to walk without tipping over was a modern-day miracle.

The one draping herself across Kyson and rubbing said bowling balls against him every chance she could get had enough horse hair in her head to qualify her for the Kentucky Derby.

"*That's* the kind of woman he likes?" Michael mumbled, wrinkling her nose as if a skunk had streaked across the table.

"What?" Sheldon asked, pulling her attention away from whatever nonsensical story their stepmother was going on about. "The kind of woman *who* likes?"

Michael nodded in Kyson's direction. "Why do men always fall for the slutty bimbos?"

"Is that a *real* question?" Frankie asked, laughing.

The sisters chuckled in response.

"What is so funny down there?" Marlin, their father, asked, wanting the girls to let him and Donna in on the joke.

"Nothing, Daddy," Michael said. "We were just trying to figure out what makes men fall for the young-bimbo type."

A hush fell over the crowd and Michael realized what her words implied, especially since her father's complexion darkened to a deep plum and Donna dropped her fork.

"Oh, I didn't mean you and Donna," she quickly apologized. "I just meant in general."

That didn't make it any better.

"I meant men who went for women half their age with fake…"

Sheldon and Joey lunged and clamped a hand over Michael's mouth.

"Excuse us for a moment," Frankie said, pushing back from her chair and directing the other sister to drag Michael along for an emergency ladies'-room huddle.

Michael had no choice but to allow her four sisters to extract her from the table and shove her across the restaurant.

"What the hell has gotten into you?" P.J. barked the moment they crossed the bathroom's threshold. "Is this what you call putting forth an effort?"

"I'm sorry." Michael flushed. "I didn't mean it the way it sounded. Really."

Four angry faces glared.

"You know what?" she said, tossing her hands up. "I should go home. It was a bad idea for me to come out tonight." She snatched her purse from Sheldon's hands. It was better for her to kick herself out of the party than to actually let one of them do it, which was just about to happen judging by their faces. "Tell Dad I'm sorry."

Michael marched out the bathroom door and pretended to be unaffected by the fact that none of her sisters tried to stop her from leaving. To add insult to injury she also had to walk past Detective Dekker's table on her way out. Pride prevented her from casting her gaze in his direction, but it didn't mean she didn't feel the detective's heavy gaze follow her out of the restaurant.

She did.

She just didn't know whether it was a good thing or not. Something told her only time would tell.

Chapter 10

The last thing Michael needed was a flat tire.

But after hearing the unmistakable thumping and feeling the constant jerk of the steering wheel, she couldn't think of a better way to cap a lousy week. Grudgingly, Michael pulled over on the Pacheco Pass. The four-lane freeway was as dark and desolate as the Nevada desert and almost just as scary.

"I swear if it wasn't for bad luck I'd have no luck at all," Michael complained. She retrieved her cell phone from her purse. Even before she looked, she suspected her bad luck would extend to her phone's inability to get a signal.

And she was right.

"Just great!" She dropped her head back on the headrest and tried to calm herself by closing her eyes and counting to ten. When that didn't work, she went to twenty.

Then thirty.

Forty.

Okay. So it finally worked when she hit one hundred. She opened her eyes and clicked on her hazard lights before she climbed out of the car to check which tire was the culprit. It was the front passenger side that was as flat as a pancake. Because of the dark, she couldn't tell what had caused the blowout, but by rubbing her hands along the tire, she could feel the tire's large gash.

"What the hell?" she swore. "I just bought these damn tires!" Michael climbed back onto her feet and expelled a long tired breath. Her eyes scanned the dark, winding road and she wondered if it would be a blessing or a curse if someone stopped to help her.

It had been years, if not decades, since she had to personally change a flat, and being in a pair of tight-tight jeans and high-heeled sandals didn't exactly tickle her fancy to change one now in the dark.

"Okay. First things first," she coached herself. "Where is the flashlight?" She opened the passenger door and dug her emergency flashlight out of the glove compartment.

A pair of headlights swept across the landscape and then rested on her.

Temporarily blinded by the spotlight, Michael shielded her eyes as caution tickled her neck. A large SUV pulled off the side of the road and parked behind her car.

Michael stood still, unsure of what to do in such a vulnerable position. *Refuse the help, get back into the car and lock the doors.*

Just as she was about to heed the voice of reason in her head, a woman's voice floated out to her.

"Do you need any help?"

Relieved, Michael relaxed and flashed the face-less woman a smile. "I have a flat."

The driver's door of the SUV opened, and this time a tall, bulky, faceless stranger stepped out. "I think we can help you with that," the man said.

"Thanks. I appreciate that," Mike said, feeling more than grateful to the kind couple. "Let me just pop the trunk. I have a jack and a spare back there."

She entered her vehicle through the passenger side, where she crawled and stretched across the seat to reach the trunk button. She heard the telltale pop and then crawled back out. However, her helpers weren't waiting for her by the trunk, they were standing behind her.

Before she had the chance to question them, the bulky stranger grabbed her from behind and muffled her scream.

"Relax, Michael," his rumbling baritone coaxed. "You know how this kidnapping thing goes."

* * *

"C'mon, Kyson," Khail said with his two favorite gold-star jump-off chicks looped on his arms. "Are you sure you want a rain check tonight? Porsche and Mercedes are ready to roll," he teased. "If you know what I mean."

"I *do* know what you mean," Kyson said, removing his credit card from his wallet. "And I'm still going to have to pass." Every year his brother took him out to dinner for his birthday, but somehow Kyson was the one left holding the check.

"All right," Khail said, sounding nonplussed about his brother's decision. "I guess that means more for me."

The girls giggled, but Mercedes, the one that spent the entire dinner rubbing on Kyson and popping bubble gum by his ear, looked disappointed.

"Sorry. Maybe next time."

An indignant Michael kicked and squirmed, confident she was going to break her captors' hold on her at any minute.

"Just get her in the trunk," the woman ordered.

"We don't have a trunk!" the man roared back.

Oh hell, no! Michael stomped her heel down hard on her captor's foot.

"Ow!" His arms loosened.

Michael pivoted and, despite the dark, delivered a high-powered kick right between the man's legs.

He hit the ground with a loud "Oomph!"

Before Michael could think about exacting revenge on the woman, something hot whizzed by her ear a millisecond before she heard a *pop!*

She's shooting at me!

Kyson rushed toward his car, trying to escape the giggling trio. "I hope the sacrifice is worth it, bro," Khail said, sliding into the passenger seat of the ditsy twins' cherry-red convertible. "But don't worry. I'll send you a postcard from heaven."

Kyson laughed and shook his head as he climbed in behind the wheel of his beloved fifteen-year-old Honda Accord. After he started the car and pulled out of the restaurant, his laugh downgraded into sporadic chuckles. It wouldn't surprise Kyson in the least if his brother left this world a dirty old man with two barely legal porn stars by his side.

Just like their grandfather.

And their father.

At least Khail was smart enough not to get married. How could he after watching the hell their mother went through, tracking down the women who'd lured their father away from home on a weekly and sometimes daily basis?

To this day, nothing unnerved Kyson more than the sound of a woman crying, which, in his line of work, happened more days than not. During his time in the department, his shoulder had soaked up its fair share of tears when he had to deliver the news of a loved one's being injured or killed in some senseless crime.

If the women weren't crying, they were angry or running around hysterically…sort of like the woman that was running up the street toward him now.

"What in the hell?" Kyson slammed down on his brakes. His tires screeched while he felt the back of his car fishtail. In the blink of an eye, he'd lost control of the car. His hands came off the steering wheel. A few heartbeats later, the car finally stopped, but he was completely turned around and would be facing oncoming traffic if he didn't hurry and get off the road.

Before he could get his senses back, the hysterical woman, who'd almost killed him, started banging the roof of his car.

"Help me! Help me!" she screamed. "They're trying to kidnap me!"

Once Kyson blinked out of his stupor, recognition settled in. *Michael Adams?*

Recognition also dawned in her eyes.

Michael raced to the other side of his car and tried the door handle, but it was locked. That sent her hysteria to a new level.

"Unlock the door! Unlock the door!"

He complied because it looked as if she was going to wrench it off the frame.

Michael flew into the car like a hurricane, but

before he could open his mouth to question her, a pair of headlights rounded the bend. Once again, she screamed.

"Move! Move! Move!"

Kyson hit the accelerator and jerked the steering wheel in a hard left. Neither of them breathed until they made it off the freeway just as an eighteen-wheeler whizzed by, leaving the Honda rocking on the side of the road.

Kyson glanced at his passenger. In less than one minute, his life had passed before his eyes—twice!

"Lady, are you crazy?" he snapped.

Wild brown eyes shot to meet his, causing him to regret his sudden outburst. That is, until she flew off the handle.

"You almost hit me," she accused.

He stared. Blinking.

"You could have killed me," she went on.

"Y-you were running up the middle of the street screaming," he stammered. Griff was right. This woman *was* crazy.

"I was running in the middle of the street because someone was trying to kidnap me," she said as if she was explaining something that actually made sense.

He stared. Blinking.

"I was running away from the kidnappers," she added. "Drive up the road. You'll see my car around the bend."

What else could he do but follow her orders?

Maybe the faster he did this, the quicker he could get her out of his car. It suddenly didn't seem like a great idea to be alone with her.

Kyson pulled onto the main freeway. His gaze strayed back to his beautiful and buxom passenger and weighed whether she was genuine, crazy or on something.

His car rounded the bend and he saw a black Volvo pulled off to the side of the road.

"See? There's my car!"

"Uh-huh," he said cautiously. "And your mysterious kidnappers?"

Michael cocked her head. "Were they supposed to wait for me to bring the cops back?"

Okay, he had that one coming. He pulled his car to a stop behind hers and cut on his own hazard lights. When it was clear she wasn't ready to step out of the car, he asked, "So what happened?"

She sank farther into the car seat and tilted her head back against the headrest. "It's all such a blur now," she admitted, pressing a hand to her forehead. "I had a flat tire so I pulled over to the side of the road. When I got out of my car, this SUV pulled over behind me." She licked her lips as if she was suddenly parched.

"Go on," he urged.

As Michael retold what had happened, a part of her had yet to wrap itself around what had actually happened. It wasn't until the cop asked, "Who do you know who would want to cause you harm?" that she finally started laughing like a crazy person. Hell, it could take all night to run down the long list of people who wanted to get even for one prank or another.

In her lifetime, she concluded that very few people had a good sense of humor. Michael laughed a good while before she realized her handsome cop couldn't possibly understand what she found so amusing.

"Let's just say that I've pulled my fair share of practical jokes."

"So this whole thing was some retaliation for a practical joke?" he said, trying to understand.

She'd almost said yes or even maybe before she realized that there was absolutely nothing funny about dodging bullets. "No. Definitely not," she said, sobering.

The detective eyed her through the faint light of the car's dashboard before making a decision. "Stay right here." He opened the driver's-side door and climbed out.

He most certainly didn't have to tell Michael twice. She watched as he walked in front of the car. His bright headlights showcased his tall, magnificent body. Almost instantly, she forgot about the danger of the past few minutes while her gaze glided appreciatively over what could only be described as a body that needed to be draped across the pages of *Playgirl* or at least across her bed.

"Lord have mercy, what I wouldn't do for a tall

glass of *that* chocolate milk." Her eyes followed him as he crouched down by her front passenger-side tire for an inspection. When he leaned in closer, she leaned forward for a better view of his butt.

Nice.

Kyson stood, walked around the car and even inspected the ground. Was he looking for the different set of tire tracks to corroborate her story? Irritation pricked her pride. Surely he believed her. Who would make up a story like this?

Finally, Kyson walked toward the car and tapped the passenger-side window.

Michael hit the power button and rolled down the window.

"I'm just going to change the tire and then I can follow you to the nearest police station so you can file a report."

"A report?" she echoed, suddenly unsure. What if Phil was simply paying her back for the other night? Wouldn't that mean she would have to tell the police she'd lied to them when they'd come asking about her missing husband?

But what about the gun? Would Phil actually try to kill her? Heck, she didn't even know whether it was a real gun, now that she thought about it.

"You know, I think I'd rather just go home," she said, dropping her gaze. She knew that she sounded like a complete flake, but suddenly the whole situation seemed too complicated.

The detective studied her for a long moment. "Ms. Adams, *if* what you say is true then I advise you to file a police report."

"Why?" she challenged. "You think they're going to believe me any more than you do?"

When he didn't answer her, she felt herself grow angry. "Just fix the tire and I'll go home."

Again, he didn't move.

"Please," she added with artificial sweetness, and batted her eyes just so, which usually had the effect of men giving her what she wanted.

"All right," he finally agreed. "But I'm following you home."

Chapter 11

No doubt about it, he was dealing with a nut job.

Kyson expelled a long, tired breath, but kept his eyes focused on the black Volvo driving ahead of him. It had only taken him a few minutes to change her flat tire, but he had to admit he was more than a little intrigued by what really happened on the side of the road.

Whatever it was, it wasn't an ordinary blowout or even a nail that had flattened a brand-new tire. Frankly, it looked as though someone had stabbed it with a knife. But why would anyone do that?

Or why did she do it?

He remembered her dramatic exit out of Nicolino's and how she didn't even glance his way. Gone was the earlier flirtation and in its place was a marching Amazon giving him the cold shoulder.

Was it possible that she'd been jealous of his brother's so-called birthday gift? He considered the possibility, but then dismissed it as wishful thinking.

Well, maybe not so wishful since it was now clear that Michael Adams needed psychiatric help.

Minutes later, he pulled into Michael's driveway and watched her as she climbed out of her car. She gave him a short wave as she slipped a purse strap over her shoulder and then turned and headed toward the front door.

"Once she's inside, put the pedal to the metal," he told himself, already shifting the gears into Reverse. However, when she reached the door, she stopped cold. He watched her for a few seconds but she remained frozen on the doorstep. "Good Lord. What is it now?"

Kyson shifted the car back into Park and then rolled down his window. "Is there a problem?"

She glanced back over her shoulder. "The door is open," she said just barely over the hum of his engine. "I *know* I locked this door when I left."

"I was right," he mumbled to himself as he shut off his engine. "Crazy is never boring." He climbed out of his car and walked toward the front door. "Are you *sure* you locked it?"

She nodded yes, but said, "I think so."

He warred with whether or not it would be rude to ask her if she was on some sort of medication, and then decided that it would be. "Do you want me to go in and check things out for you?"

It was odd that she hesitated and again he wondered what type of game this woman was playing. One minute she was afraid of her own shadow and then the next she was direct and bossy.

"It will just take me a few minutes," he said, wanting to speed things up a bit. When she looked up at him beneath the porch light, he caught the flicker of uncertainty in her dark orbs.

The muscles around his heart tightened while the ones in his pants hardened. What was it about this woman that intoxicated him so much? Why did his hands itch to run through her hair? Why did he crave her taste as though he was already addicted to it?

"Stay right here," he instructed and then pushed open the door and entered.

Michael followed his instructions—for a few seconds anyway. Coming home and finding her door unlocked stunned and threw her off her game for a moment, but now she found herself growing angry at what had to be Phil's retaliation. Did he honestly think that he could beat her at her own game?

She was the queen of revenge and practical jokes. He would have to come harder than this. She started to march into the house behind Detective Dekker when something rustled from the side bushes.

"Who's there?" she challenged and then squinted for a closer look. The night silence roared back at her while her eyes started playing tricks with light and shadows. "Phil, if that's you and your cronies, the gig is up. There's a cop here and I don't think he'll find any of this funny."

Her words melted into the night. Soon after, her anger upgraded to fury. "Phil, it's late and I'm not in the mood."

Again, silence was the night's only answer and instead of staying put on the porch, she launched her own investigation around the house.

Meanwhile, Kyson had no idea whether Ms. Adams's home had been disturbed. The place looked in the same disarray as it had been the other day. He gave the place a casual once-over and then went back out to the front porch to find it deserted.

"Now where did she go?" He glanced around, saw that her car was still parked and then started scratching his head. "Not boring at all," he mumbled under his breath and then searched around the house.

Spooked by how still and quiet the night was, Michael had trouble swallowing the lump in her throat because she expected Phil to jump out of the bushes at any moment. When she finally made it around to the pool area, she finally heard the heavy footfall of her elusive predator.

However, before she could get the drop on him, a tabby cat streaked in front of her. She jumped, screamed and lost her balance at the edge of the pool. Michael flailed her arms but she knew before her legs swept completely out from beneath her that she was going down.

A pair of hands appeared out of nowhere and she grabbed at them as a last bid to save herself. Instead, she pulled her potential savior into the pool with her. Eight feet of ice-cold water felt like a bed of needles pricking every inch of her body, but at least she had the presence of mind not to cry out or fill her lungs with the dirty chlorine water.

Now, more than ever, she regretted buying a house with a pool when she didn't know how to swim.

Something akin to steel bands wrapped around her waist and swept her upward where sweet oxygen awaited her once she broke through the water's surface. She chugged in as much as she could while trying to kick and splash her way back to the pool's edge.

"Relax. Relax," Kyson barked. "I've got you!"

Relax? How could she relax? She was drowning.

"Ms. Adams, if you don't stop, you're going to drown both of us. Now relax so I can get us out of this damn water!"

Going against her nature, she decided to trust this man. Still, she halfway expected to sink like a stone, but was relieved when they began to tread toward the metal stairs near the end of the pool.

"C'mon. Climb up."

Again, Michael did as she was told though it now felt as if her jeans weighed an extra fifty pounds—and where were her shoes?

"Wait, wait," she said, stopping halfway up the ladder. "I lost my shoes. You gotta go back in and get my shoes."

"What?" he thundered incredulously.

"You don't understand. They're Prada!"

He didn't move nor did he say anything.

He couldn't.

"Please," she added, purring.

"Fine," he said. "Just get out of the pool."

With a trembling smile, Michael finished climbing the ladder and turned in time to see Detective Dekker dive back into the pool for her precious babies. Despite feeling like a frozen Popsicle, Michael remained poolside while watching Kyson's beautiful body glide beneath the water. The man was truly poetry in motion and she was certain that magnificent body would be revisiting her tonight in her dreams.

When he broke through the water's surface with her shoes held high in his hands, she knew she was in love. Okay, maybe not in love, but certainly she had a serious case of lust. The man was a chiseled chocolate god and he'd just rescued one of her most prized possessions.

Surely that deserved a reward.

A hug.

A kiss.

Hot buck-naked sex with lots of baby oil.

Good Lord, when was the last time she'd had sex?

"Okay, I've rescued your shoes, there's no one in your house. Now I'd like to go home," Kyson said, climbing out of the pool and thrusting her shoes and her purse into her hands.

Her smile died as she pushed her wet hair from her line of vision. "But—but—"

"Good night, Ms. Adams," he said, marching off.

She turned and rushed after him. "You can't go like this. You'll catch your death in those clothes."

He stopped suddenly and she crashed into his brick wall of a back.

"Oops. Sorry," she said.

He turned and faced her. "Ms. Adams—"

"You know, considering all we've been through tonight, you really should just call me Mike."

"Ms. Adams," he insisted. "I'm going home because around you, my life seems to be in danger every ten minutes. I'll just take my chances with pneumonia."

Michael never liked losing an argument, and not getting her way only appealed to her competitive side.

Plus, she was really horny.

"Okay," she said and pulled her low-cut blouse over her head and flashed him with the sight of her large breasts nestled in a lacy pink bra.

"I just wanted you to know I have a perfectly good dryer in the house." She unsnapped the top button of her jeans and watched as his mouth sagged open.

Yeah. She still had it.

Chapter 12

Kyson wasn't thinking.

Well, not with the right head anyway.

He couldn't remember what Michael had said after she'd removed her top. His gaze had immediately dropped to the sight of her creamy caramel breasts that seemed to glow beneath the moonlight. When she turned away to walk back toward the house, he followed as if hypnotized.

There was a voice, although very faint, in the back of his head telling him to run to his car and get the hell out of there, but he ignored it and followed the sway of Michael's hips.

Entering the house, Kyson couldn't help but hesitate.

Michael stopped at the door and leaned against it with a taunting smile. "Don't worry. I won't bite… hard."

The challenge was made and Kyson's lips curled as he crossed the threshold. True, it wasn't clear exactly what Michael Adams was offering or even suggesting, but he hoped—no, prayed—that it was going to be worth his while.

Michael closed the door and turned the lock.

From over his shoulder, he glanced back in time to catch her checking him out. When her eyes crept up to finally meet his, they held another challenge that made him hard as a rock.

"Wait here," she said, heading toward the stairs. "I'll change and then bring you something so you can slip out of those clothes."

He didn't answer. He was once again hypnotized by the sway of those magnificent round hips as they ascended before him. He followed as far as the foot of the stairs, gazing up as if looking toward the heavens.

In a way, he was.

When she finally disappeared from sight and he heard the soft click of the bedroom door, he finally blinked out of his trance and wondered what in the hell he was doing. Had abstinence addled his brain?

Kyson remembered the ditsy twins and knew

that couldn't quite be it. He'd had no trouble turning down the women his brother had thrown at him, but one flash of Michael Adams's Victoria's Secret and he was practically salivating.

Would she be everything his dreams had promised? Would her skin be as soft, her mouth as intoxicating, her inner thighs...

Kyson closed his eyes, sucked in a deep breath, but still mumbled a "Lord have mercy." If he allowed his thoughts to get carried away, whatever was going to happen between them could possibly end a lot sooner than anticipated.

His fingers attacked the buttons on his shirt. He removed it and then whipped the T-shirt over his head. Kyson unbuttoned his pants and started to unzip them, when he stopped.

Michael didn't exactly say anything about having sex—more like it was implied. Wasn't it?

He replayed what had happened by the pool and then fast-forwarded to when she'd walked up the stairs. Unfortunately, there were a lot of holes in his memory—at least as far as the conversation went— and he was still unsure whether being naked when she returned was such a good idea.

Maybe he should toss a coin.

Michael raced through her bedroom like she was in the middle of a three-alarm fire, digging through drawers and boxes, searching for her best lingerie. That's if she had any that fit anymore.

It had been awhile since she had cause to wear lingerie. She and her ex were behaving like an old married couple long before they had taken their vows. Surely descending the stairs buck naked was a bit too forward.

Wasn't it?

Drawer after drawer, box after box, Michael came up empty, which heightened her frustration and killed her mood. Here she had a gorgeous man in her house with the perfect excuse to get him naked and do sinfully wicked things to him and the best thing she had to wear was…flannel.

Maybe she should just go down naked.

Naked or flannel.

She sighed.

Maybe she should toss a coin.

What was taking so long?

Kyson wondered if he was the butt of a joke, standing in a strange woman's house in wet clothes. Yet, he stood riveted at the foot of the stairs, waiting anxiously to see what heavenly creation she'd wear as she descended.

A door opened from the top floor and every muscle in Kyson's body clenched in anticipation.

"Play it cool. Play it cool," he coached himself,

trying to prop himself against the banister, determined to be as suave and debonair as Denzel.

At long last, his curvaceous angel appeared at the top of the stairs—magnificent in…flannel.

He straightened from the banister and blinked up at the vision coming toward him. True, he'd envisioned something silk, perhaps with a little lace, or even something the other way around. So he was stunned to see the red-and-black midlength flannel gown, but Kyson had to hand it to the buxom beauty: she was the only woman he'd seen who knew how to make flannel *sexy*.

He lowered his gaze and then worked his way up from her bright red painted toes to where a thin gold chain with the letter M bounced against her left ankle; his gaze then slid up thick, creamy brown calves that led the way to even thicker creamier thighs.

Blood raced from one head to the other at a speed that left him dizzy. Michael's short gown clearly outlined the dangerous curves of her body, as well as hinted of sweet promises of pleasure. By the time he took in her sly smile and her twinkling gaze, he knew resistance was futile.

Michael stopped before him. "Let's see if we can get you out of those clothes now." She pressed a robe to his chest and made sure her right breast brushed against his arm as she stepped off the last stair and sashayed around him.

Of course he followed, pulling and unbuttoning clothes as fast as he could. He nearly fell on his face, trying to get one leg out of his pants, leaving him to hop halfway through the living room. He was almost panting by the time he reached the laundry room off from the kitchen.

Michael opened the top of the washing machine and turned toward him and stopped. It was the only thing she could do when fantasy crashed with reality. Quite frankly, fantasy paled in comparison.

This was no couch-potato cop with a donut belly. This man looked as if he was born and raised in a gym. Large and small mountains of muscle stood proud along his shoulders and arms, while his abs looked like rippling waves of chocolate.

"My, my, my," she said, still smiling when he handed over his clothes and then slipped into the soft terry-cloth robe that, surprisingly, fit.

"I bought it as a birthday gift for my brother," she explained. "It's coming up."

"I hope he doesn't mind," he said.

"But tonight is your birthday, right?"

He nodded.

She dumped his clothes in. "Then I guess I should see about giving you something…special." She held out her hand.

He looked down, wondering what she was asking for.

"Aren't you forgetting something?" she prompted.

He swallowed. At this moment, he wouldn't be able to tell her his name if she asked.

"Your boxers," she said. "Surely you don't think I'm going to let you walk around in wet boxers?"

He'd hoped not, but he was still unsure what was and wasn't appropriate. Quickly, Kyson decided to err on the side of caution and tied the robe closed before sliding out of his underwear, but he did do so with his eyes locked on Michael's.

Her smile inched higher before she glanced down. "Ooh, Armani. On a cop's salary?"

Heat scorched its way up Kyson's neck. "They were a gift from my sister," he said.

"Sister?" She placed the boxers in the washing machine, threw in some detergent and started it. "Do you have any idea how sad it sounds that your sister buys your underwear?"

He chuckled. "You said this robe was for your brother."

Mike shrugged. "That's different."

"How?" he barked, incredulous.

"My brother is gay."

Kyson's laughter faded.

"I guess my first question should be—are you gay?"

He started laughing again. "No."

"Bisexual?"

"No."

"On the down low?"

"No." He captured her gaze again and then moved toward her until her breasts pressed against his chest and his steel-rod erection pressed against her soft belly. "I'm one hundred percent straight. I love women." His gaze traveled down to where he had a damn good view of the double D's she was carrying. "I especially love voluptuous beauties who tease too much."

Kyson, in a startling move, picked Michael up and sat her on top of the washing machine. "Now suppose we stop all this playing around and get down to business?"

She didn't respond, but he certainly had her attention. Brute strength had that effect on her.

It also had a way of turning her on.

"What are we doing here tonight?" he asked, standing in between her legs. "Did you really bring me in here so you could dry my clothes or…" Kyson leaned forward and brushed his lips against hers like a feather. "Are we going to play games all night?"

This was the moment Michael had been waiting for since Detective Fine showed up at her door. Now that it was here, she didn't feel so confident.

She was giddy.

Hot.

Nervous.

"Maybe we should start off by removing this," he said, playing with the hem of her gown. He allowed a few seconds of silence to lapse, plenty of time for her to say no.

When she didn't, he pulled the gown up and over her head. He was blown away by the glorious vision before him. Rich, luscious feminine curves beckoning for his touch, caress and kiss.

And he was anxious to get started.

Pleasure rushed through Michael at seeing Kyson's open approval. So much so, she could feel her confidence dripping back into her blood. She deserved a hot, onetime fling, didn't she?

Her love life didn't need to end because she was staring down the barrel at forty and was divorced. She was still a woman with needs; needs that had been ignored for far too long.

Michael reached behind her back and unsnapped her bra.

Kyson gasped, stared for what felt like eternity before his strong hands roamed up her thighs, up the sides of her hips and then finally over to cup her full breasts.

She gasped, quivered and pulled his head forward so she could ravish his lips in a hungry kiss.

Instead it was he who ravished her.

From the moment his tongue delved into her mouth, she was lost. He tasted like Godiva and was as intoxicating as the strongest brandy. And good Lord, she loved the way the pads of his fingers kept circling her hard nipples.

Delicious.

He was the first to break the kiss, giving her time to drag precious air into her lungs. He lifted one of her breasts and locked his lips around the tip.

Michael's head eased back while her eyes closed so she could concentrate on his soft suckling and she could peel the new robe from his shoulders.

Kyson marveled at how the angel before him tasted even better than he'd ever imagined. He took his time with each marble-size nipple. Her long winding moans drove him wild, and with barely a thought in his head, he dragged her panties off her hips and down her legs and pulled her body to the edge of the machine.

"Open up for me," he ordered.

Michael eagerly complied, loving how this man took control. It was refreshing.

Though she knew what was coming and even braced for it, she still sighed and melted when his long, strong fingers slid in between her legs and brushed along her clit.

"Damn, you're hot…and wet." He panted. "You taste wonderful," he added, seizing her lips and sliding in a second finger.

Michael didn't know how he'd done it, but tears surfaced out of nowhere while her body hummed in sync with the strokes of his fingers. The washing machine rocked beneath her.

Kyson couldn't remember seeing anything more

beautiful than when Michael's lips separated from his. Her eyes remained closed while she took in three sharp breaths and trembled with the release of her first orgasm.

Wallet. Wallet. Where was his wallet?

He glanced around and saw the folded leather on the laundry-room floor. He picked it up, untied his belt and allowed the robe to fall.

"Stop," she said.

He froze and feared that this would be the end.

"I want to see every inch of you," she said. She was already more than pleased at what she saw. Kyson Dekker was a cop who packed some major heat as she guesstimated nearly double digits in length size. "Turn around."

A lone chuckle fell from his lips as his eyes rolled skyward. "I'm not a model."

"Maybe you should be," she suggested. Her eyes roamed over every ripple of muscle on his dark body. "I swear you look good enough to eat."

"Funny. I was just thinking the same about you," he responded, moving toward her again. "Spread your legs and lean back."

Michael looked over her shoulder. There was hardly any room for her to lie all the way back on the washing machine. "Maybe we should take this upstairs," she said. When she turned back to face him, she found him, standing just a few inches from her face.

"We'll get there…in due time. Now, be a good girl and do what you're told." He removed a condom from his wallet and then placed the wallet down on the dryer.

Oh, yeah. She loved how he took control.

She leaned back. The lower half of her body found room on the sparse space of the machine while part of her shoulders, neck and head rested against the back wall. Any thoughts of complaining were erased when Kyson leaned forward, brushed another kiss against her lips and then slowly worked his way down.

The man's tongue was poetry in motion, bathing her nipples while his fingers glided back inside of her. By the time he'd made it to her naval, she was breathless. When his chin brushed against soft, springy curls, Michael draped her shapely legs over his shoulders and prepared for liftoff.

Kyson was practically salivating when his fingers parted her honeyed lips and uncovered her pink jewel. The first taste of her was shockingly sweet and heavily addictive. After a few licks, Michael's knees clamped against his head while her body trembled around his stroking tongue.

No matter how much she squirmed, begged or tried to push him away, Kyson kept lapping her juices until another orgasm crested and then slammed into her and left her tingling all over.

"Please. Please," Michael panted.

At long last granting her mercy, Kyson straightened up with a smile and grabbed the Magnum condom from the top of the dryer and slid it on while Michael still languished in the aftermath of her last orgasm.

Loving her serene look, Kyson leaned forward and stole what started to be a quick kiss. It instead turned into a deep soul-stirring mating of their mouths. While he shared the taste of her honey, he pushed into her remarkably tight vaginal walls.

He was unprepared for how tight her muscles clamped around him—unprepared for how they would grip and release seemingly with very little effort on her part.

"Oh, Jesus," he groaned, fearful he would come before he could get halfway in. "Oh, Jesus."

She shifted her body and this time he was the one begging. "Don't move. Please don't move."

Michael stilled, giving him all the time he needed. Despite the condom, she was certain she could feel every vein and muscle along his long, thick shaft and was sure another orgasm would erupt before his first stroke.

Actually, it took three strokes.

Lord. How did he make each orgasm more powerful than the last?

Kyson finally caught his breath, but was slowly losing his mind. The heat of her body, the sight of her bouncing breasts and the taste of her skin consumed him and transformed his smooth even strokes into fierce hammering. Between him and the unbalanced washload, the washing machine was rocking and rolling against the floor and the back wall.

Unable to hold back any longer, Kyson swept Michael up and bounced his voluptuous goddess against his hips. The laundry room was a sauna and their bodies had become slick with sweat. Forced to prop his new lover back onto the machines before they crashed to the floor, Kyson buried his face between Michael's lush breasts while his roar of release sounded inhuman.

For a full minute afterward, Kyson and Michael dragged in huge gulps of air while they waited for their heartbeats to slow down. Despite having climaxed, Kyson's erection hadn't softened.

"Um, I think the clothes are ready for the dryer," Michael laughed.

Kyson's body vibrated with laughter. "Is that your way of saying you're not through with me?"

Michael's beautiful lips parted. "Fine, athletic and smart," she said, pinching his butt cheeks. "I'm starting to think it's *my* birthday."

He kissed her. "Then why don't we move this birthday party up to your bedroom?"

"What—not the closet?"

"Don't tempt me."

Michael dutifully hopped off the machine, removed Kyson's clothes from the washer and put them into the dryer before leading her Adonis up to her bedroom where she proceeded to wear his butt out.

Chapter 13

Michael smiled as she stretched along the cotton sheets of her queen-size bed. She couldn't remember the last time she'd felt so glorious, so satisfied and so drained. What happened last night cast a different light on her past relationships. Until now, she had no idea of what she was missing.

She had been so caught up wanting the title of Mrs. Somebody that she never thought she was selling herself short. Sure, sex with her ex had been good, but what she'd experienced with Kyson went further than that.

Sex with Detective Dekker was fantastic.

"Sweetheart?"

"Hmm?" she responded with her eyes still closed while drifting on the lofty clouds in her head.

"Don't you think it's about time you uncuffed me?"

Michael's lashes fluttered open and she stared into eyes that were as dark and rich as black coffee. The fact that he wore a smile that matched hers told her that he, too, had had a wonderful night, despite her having fallen asleep with him still handcuffed to her headboard.

"Do you remember what we did with the key?" she asked, curling into him and pressing her hand against his flat stomach.

The moment she touched him, it shot off another spark, and judging by the way the sheet over his hips raised, she knew he'd felt it, as well.

"It's on the bed around here somewhere."

"Oh?" Her hand drifted down and slid beneath the sheet. "Maybe I should look for it down here." Michael's hand wrapped around his swollen member and gave it a little squeeze.

Kyson sucked in air while his eyes slid closed.

Loving his response to her touch, Michael leaned forward and kissed him full on the mouth. The hundredth kiss was just as potent as the first and had the effect of wiping her mind clean of any trouble.

When she came up for air, she finally had to ask him the one thing that had been heavy on her mind. "How is it that a man like you is still single?"

He opened his mouth, but then closed it when she gave his erection another playful squeeze.

"Be warned. It's in your best interest to tell the truth," she said.

He laughed. "I was married once," he admitted. "Years ago. Right after high school, in fact."

Michael released him, not because of what he said, but because of the tone in his voice. Sadness? Longing? Regret?

"What happened?"

Now he had a hard time looking at her.

In a snap, Michael felt as if another woman had entered the bed with them and no amount of reasoning could tame her sudden surge of jealousy.

"She was killed in a drive-by shooting," he said.

Michael's body slumped in sorrow and she was ashamed of her jealousy. "I'm sorry. I didn't know."

His lips curled a bit, but he still didn't meet her stare. "It's been nearly ten years and it scares me sometimes that I can barely remember…" He shook his head. "The day she was killed changed my life. I dropped out of college and joined the police force, thinking that I would be the one to solve her murder. I was going to be the one that brought justice to such a senseless death."

"Did you?" she asked.

"The police caught him, if that's what you mean." He shook his head. "But justice is another thing entirely."

"Who was it?"

"Some punk's initiation into some gang," he answered. "One of his boys rolled on him to cut a better deal in a convenience-store robbery. Turns out the kid's parents had long pockets, good friends and pretty damn good lawyers."

"He got off?"

Kyson sighed. "Turns out Lady Justice can be a high-stakes hooker sometimes. She pedals her wares to the highest bidder."

Silence lapsed between them. One of the few times Michael was speechless.

"I guess the reason I haven't gotten married again is because it took me a long time to get over what I lost. And when I finally did, I realized…that there are a lot of crazy women out here."

Michael laughed. "Well, you know, some say that I'm a little…eccentric."

"Oh?" he asked. "I would have never guessed."

Michael's eyes narrowed. "Are you being sarcastic?" She squeezed him again and in response his erection returned.

"A little," he admitted. "But I guess a little crazy is all right."

Giggling, Michael captured another kiss and even nibbled a bit on his bottom lip. "Good answer, copper."

He joined in on her laughter.

"I do have one more question for you," she said.

"Shoot."

"Are you sure you're over your wife?" Actually, she didn't even know why she was asking. This was supposed to be a fling—a little something to get her back into the swing of being single. Why was she sitting there interviewing him for a more serious position?

His hesitation lasted so long Michael feared she'd broken a rule of one-night stands. "Look," she said, searching for a way to save face. "Don't answer that. I don't even know why I asked."

"I hope you asked because you're thinking about seeing me again," he said.

She certainly was.

"And my answer is, I don't think anyone truly gets over their first love, doubly so when you lose them under such tragic circumstances. But I have to honestly say that time, that life is over. I loved her, I lost her and I mourned her. Perhaps longer than necessary, but I am looking to start living again."

Kyson didn't realize how true his words were until they started tumbling out of his mouth. Then again, he hadn't expected to feel the things he felt while lying next to her, either. Talking to Michael felt easy. Natural.

Even after a night of unbelievable sex, electricity crackled between them.

It didn't make sense. He was like the Energizer Bunny around her. He couldn't get enough.

"Now," he said, trying to bring back their previous jovial mood, "what do you say we get back to looking for that key?"

Michael's full lips split into another wide smile as her hand gave up squeezing for long sensual strokes. "Do you mean this key?"

"Oh, Lord," Kyson sighed, sinking deep into the bed's plush padding.

"You like that, do you?" she purred. With her other free hand she peeled the sheet from his hips. One look at his beautiful black shaft and her body tingled again. "You know, I still owe you a favor," she said.

Kyson quirked a brow, but when Michael inched her way down his body, he knew exactly what she had in mind.

"You know you don't have to do that," he said, giving her an out.

"I know," she whispered. Her warm breath drifted across his straining flesh. "I only do things I want to do." She kissed the tip and then flicked her tongue against the same spot.

Kyson quivered while his breathing thinned in his chest. He wanted to run his hands through her hair while she took him into her mouth, but all he could do was pull at his handcuffs and chafe his wrists.

"I'm in control of this groove," she said.

And control it she did. She took her time working her mouth over his sex. Slipping and sliding and working him into a frenzy. A few times, he tried to take over by pumping his hips, but Michael would punish him by pulling away.

It was maddening.

It was wonderful.

It was heaven.

A minute later, Kyson stopped breathing, squeezed his eyes tight and watched fireworks explode behind his eyelids.

And Michael was just getting started.

When she finally uncuffed him both were bruised in places they never thought possible. When they finally pried themselves out of bed both walked on legs that trembled and threatened to collapse.

"I'm going to go downstairs and start a pot of coffee," she told him.

"You're coming back up to join me in the shower?"

She lifted a questioning brow.

"What?" he asked. "You wash my back and I'll wash yours."

"Sounds like an offer I can't refuse." She shrugged one shoulder and winked before finally escaping her bedroom. However, as she made her journey down to the kitchen, Kyson and the wonderful hours they'd had together kept repeating in her mind.

Every moment they'd shared seemed like a dream—one she wished would never end. When she entered the kitchen, she was singing Carl Carlton's "She's a Bad Mama Jama" and rocking her hips to the groove.

As was her habit, she turned on the small television on the counter, catching the looping news on CNN.

"The body was discovered by two local teenagers hiking up Pacheco Pass…"

Bam! Bam! Bam!

"Who in the hell?" Michael hit the brew button on the coffee machine, tightened the belt on her robe and went to see who was trying to break down her door. One thing for sure, it wouldn't be the police. Detective Fine was waiting for her in her shower.

Bam! Bam! Bam!

"I'm coming. I'm coming," she snapped and then frowned at the déjà vu moment. "Who is it?"

"Just open the damn door," Sheldon snapped.

What on earth got her panties in a wad?

Michael jerked open the door, but before she could bark out a question her sisters burst inside like a runaway locomotive.

"Girl, have you seen the news?" Frankie asked, taking the lead.

"Please, please, tell us that you had nothing to do with this," P.J. begged, bringing up the rear, both hands pressed into her back as she waddled into the living room.

"What the hell are you guys talking about?" Michael closed the door and then followed.

"We mean it this time," Joey said, picking up the television remote. "If you're behind this, tell us now. We'll get you the best lawyer money can buy."

"Lawyer?" Michael repeated, struggling to keep up with the conversation. "Why would I need a lawyer?"

Joey turned up the television.

"The police have confirmed the body to be that of forty-year-old African-American businessman Philip Matthews of San Jose."

"What?" Michael's head whipped toward the television. "What?"

"We've been able to confirm that Mr. Matthews was reported missing three days ago," the reporter said. "According to the missing person's report, a Ms. Delaney insisted that Matthews's ex-wife was behind his unexplained disappearance. We're currently trying to confirm whether the San Jose Police Department had followed up on the report and we're also trying to reach Ms. Delaney for further questioning."

"What?" Michael thundered.

"Will you please say something else," Frankie snapped.

"I can't," Michael admitted honestly. "There has to be some kind of mistake. Phil isn't dead," she said, blood rushing from her head. "He can't be."

Joey punched the mute button on the television. "Are you saying that you had *nothing* to do with this?"

Michael's head jerked up. "Of course that's what I'm saying! How in the hell could you all think I could be a murderer?"

"Until three days ago we didn't think you were a kidnapper, either. But you have a knack for surprising us," Sheldon said.

"I don't believe this," Michael said. "I need to sit." She moved to the sofa and plopped down.

"Hell, I need a Valium," Frankie said.

"All right. All right," Sheldon said, pacing. "Let's not panic."

"Not panic?" Peyton echoed, dropping next to Michael on the sofa. "You guys lied to the police. That's bound to get out—especially when you have two idiots like Ray and Scott Damon out there. If they left any traceable evidence in that house, the cops are going to pick them up. They pick them up, they are going to roll on Mike. They'll roll on their own momma and you know it. They'll say Mikey hired them. A kidnapping you lied about. If they nail her for kidnapping it's not too far a leap to charge her with murder."

Michael groaned.

"Thanks," Sheldon said. "We all feel much better now, P.J."

"I'm just saying this situation can't possibly get any worse."

The sound of someone walking down the stairs caught everyone's attention. "Hey, baby. I thought you were going to join me in the shower…" Kyson stepped into the living room and froze before he flashed them a smile of embarrassment. "Oh. Hello, ladies."

Peyton said, "I stand corrected."

Chapter 14

Thinking quickly, Frankie grabbed the remote from Joey and shut off the television.

"Isn't that the robe we chipped in for for Flex's birthday?" Sheldon asked, pointing to their baby brother's sobriquet scrawled across Kyson's heart.

Michael groaned as she sank her head deep into her palms.

"Uh, since I see you're a little busy," Kyson said, backing up, "I'll just go back upstairs and, uh…get dressed."

Michael didn't answer. She just kept her face buried in her hands.

Sheldon crossed her arms and answered for her

younger sister. "Yeah…why don't you go do that, *Detective Dekker.*"

"Oookay," he said. His confusion at her hostility was visible in his expression.

Three sets of eyes followed him out of the room and then rounded toward Michael, who apparently thought if she covered her face it somehow made her invisible.

"Well?" Frankie said. "Don't tell me that a cat has finally made off with your tongue."

BAM! BAM! BAM!

Michael leaped to her feet while her heart bottomed out. "Oh my God! Who do you think that is?" she asked and then grabbed Joey's arm.

"Something tells me that it's not the Publisher's Clearing House," Peyton said, pushing herself up on her feet.

BAM! BAM! BAM!

"Mikey, baby. You want me to get the door?" Kyson asked.

"No!" she shouted and raced out of the living room.

Her sisters stayed behind and looked at each other. "Mikey, baby?" they echoed.

Kyson frowned when Michael rushed into the foyer and had barely stepped out of the way before she ran him over.

She then planted herself before the door with her arms splayed wide. "I got this. Why don't you just go on upstairs and get dressed?"

Kyson's frown deepened. "Is everything all right?"

"What? Oh, yeah. Everything is peachy keen. Why do you ask?"

BAM! BAM! BAM!

"Ms. Adams, it's the police. Please open up."

Kyson's expression melted and blocks of stone erected in its place. "Move out of the way, Michael."

"No," she said pitifully.

Her four sisters tiptoed into the foyer. Everyone's eyes darted around, waiting to see what was going to happen next.

"Ms. Adams!" the officer shouted. "We can stand here all day if you want."

"Michael," Kyson said sternly but patiently. "If you don't answer the door, I will."

Michael's arms fell to her sides as her body deflated in defeat. Why did they ever get out of bed or, better yet, why had she uncuffed him from the headboard?

BAM! BAM! BAM!

Sighing, she turned around. "All right. All right. Hold your horses," she complained and then opened the door. Immediately, her eyes flew to Detective Griffin, but this time he stood on her porch with a different partner—a thick-boned Latina with shaded eyes, crimson-stained lips and a hard jawline that made it clear she didn't take crap from anyone.

On any other day, Michael might have liked her.

"Can I help you?" Michael asked through a divided space that was just wide enough for her to poke her head through.

Griffin flashed his badge and looked as sour as his new partner. "Yes, Ms. Adams, we met three days ago? I was here asking you about your missing husband."

"Ex," she corrected out of habit.

"Right," he pushed out through clenched teeth. "We've come back to ask you a few more... I don't know if you've heard—"

"I just saw the news," she interrupted.

"Ms. Adams," his impatient partner cut in. "Can we come in? We need to talk about a rather delicate matter," she said matter-of-factly.

Michael definitely didn't want to let them in, but didn't see where she really had a choice. Intuition told her that either Kyson or her sisters would push her out of the way and invite them inside. If for no other reason than to pay her back for all the times she had butted into their business.

Damn it.

"Ms. Adams?"

Taking a deep breath, Michael finally relented and stepped back, pulling the door with her to allow them to enter.

Detective Griffin crossed the threshold first, but pulled up short when his eyes crashed into Dekker. "Kyson."

"Griff." He looked at the rookie. "Selena."

Selena Martinez actually burst out laughing. "Oh, this is rich." Her eyes darted around the crowded foyer. "Starting up your own harem, Dekker, or do you normally sleep with murder suspects on your day off?"

"Murder?" he thundered.

"Suspect?" Michael's sisters shouted at the same time.

Now six sets of eyes shot to Michael. "What?" she asked defensively. "I didn't kill him."

No one said anything.

"Frankie," Michael said, anticipating the feel of a different set of handcuffs. "I think I'm going to need those lawyers."

"Did you have to kill him?" the woman asked.

"Is it my fault the man had weak bones?" the man snapped. "Besides, we've been more than patient with him. We had to show him we meant business."

His partner swore and rolled her eyes. "But now we don't have the prototype or the money. When we show our faces to our bosses we're going to join Philip Matthews's body at the morgue."

"It's not going to come to that," he assured, picking up his binoculars to stare down the street at the unmarked police car outside Michael Adams's residence.

"Matthews didn't tell us exactly where our

package is, but he gave us enough clues to get us started."

"After that fiasco last night, I doubt we'll get anywhere near her—especially now that Matthews's body has been found. Cops are going to be crawling all over her."

"We'll get to her," he promised. "Where there's a will there's a way."

Chapter 15

The San Jose Police Department was the last place Kyson wanted to be on his vacation. And being raked across the coals about his indiscretion with Michael Adams—a *person of interest* in her ex-husband's murder case—would be a major blemish on his spotless record.

"Please try to make me understand," Captain Rex Harris said with obvious pained restraint. "Go slow on the part where you thought it was okay to engage in sexual relations with a woman you questioned about an open missing person's case."

The heat rising up Kyson's neck transformed into a blazing inferno by the time it reached his face. "No disrespect, Captain, but my personal life is my business."

"I beg to differ, Detective," Harris growled. "This is beyond whether you two are consenting adults. The fact that you met Ms. Adams during your investigation of her husband's—"

"Ex-husband," Kyson corrected.

Harris slapped both hands against his desk and leaned forward. "Don't test my patience, Dekker."

Kyson straightened in his chair, his temper barely in check. He knew his behavior with Michael last night breached no protocol. Questioning someone in a simple missing person's inquiry was not the same as seducing a primary suspect in a murder case—which, unfortunately, was increasingly turning out to be the case. Last night was complicated enough without throwing murder into the mix.

"Sir," Kyson said as diplomatically as he could muster. "I know this is a bit awkward for the department—"

"You think?" Harris snapped.

"But if this is a matter of confirming Ms. Adams's whereabouts last night, we were both at Nicolino's for dinner."

"Nice choice for a first date," Harris drawled.

"We were with different parties, sir. I was celebrating my birthday with my brother and two, uh, friends, while Ms. Adams was at the back of the restaurant with her family. I believe she said it was her father's wedding anniversary."

"And you saw this, did you?"

"Yes, sir. When she saw me, she came over and said hello."

"Mighty convenient."

"Sir, I saw when Ms. Adams left the restaurant around ten-thirty. It couldn't have been more than twenty minutes later when I also left the restaurant. I came across her, um, sort of stranded on Pacheco Pass."

"Pacheco Pass, you say?" Harris said. "That's interesting."

"Sir?"

"Well, it just so happens that Mr. Matthews's body was discovered off Pacheco Pass—near the reservoir."

Kyson blinked.

"I take it you didn't know that. Don't you watch the news?"

Kyson cleared his throat, his gaze darting away. "No, sir. I didn't get a chance to see the news this morning. I was…we were, um…"

"Busy," Harris filled in. "Yes, I got that much. Please, continue."

Kyson cleared his throat. "Well, when I came across Ms. Adams, she was a bit hysterical."

"Hysterical?"

Kyson licked his lips, knowing that his story was

about to get a little strange. "Yes, sir. She was running up the highway saying…" He cleared his throat, but still hesitated to go on.

"Saying what, Detective?"

"That…someone was trying to kidnap her."

Someone must have turned up the heat. Captain Harris's small office suddenly felt like a sauna. Kyson wouldn't have been surprised if small beads of sweat had appeared along his forehead.

In all the years he'd interrogated perpetrators, suspects and uncooperative witnesses, this was Kyson's first time in the hot seat himself.

"Someone tried to kidnap her," the captain repeated as if he feared his hearing had failed.

"Yes, sir."

Harris stood up straight and crossed his arms. "And what did you do when Ms. Adams informed you of this?"

Kyson again cleared his throat. "I drove up a stretch to where her car was located and then checked the perimeter."

"And did you see these mysterious kidnappers?"

"Uh, no, sir. I just saw her car on the side of the road with a flat tire."

"A flat tire?"

"Yes, sir. But I did notice the flat was a bit suspicious. It looked as if it had been slashed as opposed to being a blowout or the result of wear and tear."

"Then what did you do, Detective?"

"I checked the area and then changed the flat. To be honest with you, I did think that she was behaving rather…"

"Odd?" Harris supplied for him.

Kyson didn't know how to answer that—not that he wanted to.

Captain Harris chuckled. "Detective, Ms. Adams has a long history with our department. I have always found her *more* than a little odd. But please, don't leave me hanging with this delightful little story."

"Like I said, I changed the flat and then followed her home."

"Let me get this right. A woman was screaming hysterically and running up a dark highway saying that someone was trying to kidnap her and you simply changed her flat and followed her home?"

"Yes, sir."

"You didn't think to bring her in to file a report?"

"I tried to get her to come in a file to report, but she refused."

"And you didn't find that strange?"

"At the time, sir, I did find it strange." Kyson shifted in his chair.

"Uh-huh. So you followed her home, she poured you a drink and you guys fell into bed, I suppose? No offense but this sounds like a plot to a very bad skin flick."

Kyson didn't know how he remained seated. At

this very moment, he would have liked nothing more than to knock the smug look off Harris's face and then go wring Michael Adams's very lovely neck. Then again, it didn't have to be in that exact order. "It wasn't quite like that."

"No?"

"When we arrived at her place, Ms. Adams stated that her door was open and she swore she'd locked it before she left."

"Meaning?"

"Meaning that she feared there was an intruder on the premises."

"Wow. The plot thickens."

"I then went into the home and looked around."

"Let me guess," the captain said. "There was no one there."

"No, sir."

"Again, Ms. Adams decided to forgo filing a report?"

Kyson's answer struggled to fall from his lips. "Yes, sir. That's correct."

"And did you find *this* behavior odd?"

"Sir, I'm starting to find some of this line of questioning offensive."

"Good Lord." Harris tossed up his hands. "I certainly don't want to offend you."

The sarcastic tone silenced Kyson.

Captain Harris finally sat in his seat, his eyes locked on—up until now—one of his best detectives. "As you stated, this does put the department in an awkward position."

"Yes, sir. I understand I won't be assigned to the case."

"I wish it was just that simple." Harris huffed.

"I don't understand," Kyson said. "I'm Ms. Adams's alibi for last night."

"Yes. That would be all well and good if Matthews was killed last night."

Kyson blinked. "Sir?"

"According to early reports from the coroner, Philip Matthews has been dead for at least seventy-two hours."

Kyson's heart sank like lead.

"I hate to do this, Detective Dekker, but effective immediately you are suspended until further notice. Please hand over your badge."

Michael Adams's luck went from bad to worse.

Phil was dead. She drew in a deep breath and shook her head. No matter how many times those words repeated in her head, her heart had a hard time accepting it. Despite the rocky marriage, the ugly divorce and, of course, that little kidnapping thing, Michael still had feelings for her ex.

She might not have been still *in* love with him, but she still loved him—if that made any sense. Kyson had it right. You never really fall out of love with your first.

"Don't worry, Ms. Adams," Ernest Billingsley

said, patting her on the arm. "Everything is going to be all right. This is just a routine questioning. We'll give them a statement and then we'll leave."

Michael glanced over at her new lawyer—the best that money could buy according to Frankie. Michael had her doubts. First off, the man looked as if he'd slept in his suit for the past week, while one side of his face still had little dabs of styptic paper from where he'd cut himself shaving. Could the man not afford an electric razor?

If this was Frankie's idea of a joke, Michael swore she'd kill her. She closed her eyes and groaned at her poor choice of words. The last time she swore to kill someone, he *did* turn up dead.

Michael fidgeted in her chair. Her fingers drummed along the interrogation table while her legs jumped like a runaway jackhammer.

"What's taking them so long?" she asked.

"Patience," Billingsley said. "This is their way of psyching you out. They put you in a small room with nothing to eat or drink, crank up the room's temperature and then watch you sweat."

"Well, it's a good tactic," Michael complained, glancing toward the long panel of glass Billingsley had indicated.

Billingsley eyed her, undoubtedly wondering whether his new client was innocent or guilty of murder. It was a look she was rapidly getting accustomed to.

Twenty minutes later, the door to the interrogation room finally burst open and Detectives Griffin and Martinez calmly strolled inside. Neither cop said anything as they made their way over to the table. They took their time pulling back their chairs and then placing the digital recorder in between the two parties.

Detective Martinez had removed her sunglasses. This time, Michael stared into eyes the shade of black glass. Yeah. Detective Martinez was going to be the one playing bad cop.

She turned on the recorder, gave the date and time of the interview, and then finally gave Michael her full attention.

"Ms. Adams, we want to thank you for volunteering to come in here today for this interview. As you know, we are investigating the homicide of your husband, Philip Matthews."

"Ex-husband," Michael and Billingsley corrected.

Detective Griffin rolled his eyes, but still a smile curled his lips. Guess that confirmed his role as good cop.

"Ms. Adams," Martinez said, clearly impatient to get started. "Why don't you state for us the last time you saw your *ex*-husband alive."

A long silence filled the room. The first question and Michael was already in trouble. How could she admit that the last time she'd seen Phil he was tied up in the back of her Volvo?

"Um, two weeks ago," she lied.

The two cops remained silent, their hard gazes calling her the liar she was.

"Ms. Adams, you told both Detective Griffin and Detective Dekker when they spoke to you a few days ago that you had been stalking your ex in previous months, is that not correct?"

"No, ma'am," Michael said. "I wasn't stalking, I was spying."

Griffin's smile ballooned wider. "Do you mind clarifying the difference?" he asked.

"Stalking has an evil intent. I was spying for information pertaining to my divorce. I was convinced that Phil was seeing someone else. You and Detective Dekker confirmed that information for me a few days ago."

"Ms. Adams, do you normally *spy* on people?" Martinez asked.

Michael shrugged her shoulders and thought that it would be okay to admit the truth on this one. "Sometimes."

Billingsley groaned. "Can we please stick to the point? My client just came in to give a statement. She wanted it on record that she had nothing to do with her ex-husband's murder. Though she and Mr. Matthews had a rocky marriage, it ended amicably. The terms of her divorce have been finalized. Ms. Adams had no motive to kill her ex-husband."

"Why, sure she does," Detective Martinez said, smiling for the first time. "She just admitted that she'd suspected Philip Matthews of cheating, and that my partner and Detective Dekker had confirmed this information to her just days ago. Sounds like motive to me."

"Again," Billingsley said, "my client has said she had nothing to do with Matthews's murder."

Martinez turned her attention back to Michael. "Ms. Adams, you frequent a place called the Peppermill?"

Michael's mouth went dry.

"What does that have to do with anything?" Billingsley asked.

"Just answer the question," Martinez directed.

"Yes," Michael nearly spat. "I am a regular there."

"When was the last time you were there?"

"Four days ago."

"What were you doing there?"

"Celebrating my divorce. I've already told this to Detective Griffin and his previous partner."

"You mean Detective Dekker. Your current lover?"

Okay, now Michael wanted to scratch this bitch's eyes out. "That is correct." Michael straightened her spine.

"Right," Martinez said. "When you were out celebrating, did you tell everyone who would listen that you wanted to kill your ex-husband?"

Michael didn't immediately answer. She just glared at the evil woman. She just wanted five minutes with the chick in a dark alley. "I don't recall."

Now Billingsley shifted his heavy weight in his chair. "I'm sorry, but we're going have to end this interview right now."

"But we're just getting started," Martinez said.

"My client has nothing further to say."

Why hadn't he stopped the interview ten minutes ago?

Billingsley pushed himself up out of the chair. "Ms. Adams." His tone told her to get up, as well.

The man didn't have to tell her twice. Michael shot out of her seat like lightning.

Griffin leaned over the table and shut off the recorder. "Ms. Adams, we're going to have to ask you not to make any trips out of town. At least not until this matter is resolved."

Michael gave a faint nod and then followed her attorney out of the interrogation room where the air conditioner sent her a welcoming cool breeze.

As she walked through the precinct, it felt as if every eye was trained on her. One set in particular caught her attention. Glancing across the room, her gaze found Kyson's.

Their eyes locked for an instant. She couldn't tell whether the stony look was hate, disappointment or even regret. It didn't matter; it broke her heart just the same.

Lifting her chin, Michael turned away and with as much dignity as she could muster walked out.

Chapter 16

Kyson didn't like being made a fool. As he packed up the few belongings he kept in his desk, he kept going over the information Captain Harris gave him. What were the odds of Michael's ex-husband's body being discovered at the same location she had supposedly broken down? It had to be something like a million to one.

Had she just dumped the body when he'd come upon her? He thought for a moment. Surely dumping a dead man's body wasn't something that she could have done alone.

What about those so-called kidnappers?

Kidnappers or cohorts?

Sisters?

No. Couldn't have been them. They were still at the restaurant when he left. Then again, maybe they didn't dump the body last night. It could have been any time during the four days Matthews had been missing.

Was last night a complete sham? Had she made up the whole story about breaking down and someone trying to kidnap her? Now, in the light of day, it all seemed not only impossible, but unlikely. He'd walked right into her trap. Hadn't he?

He weighed that for a moment. Maybe that part truly had been a coincidence. Maybe she was just looking for anyone to be an alibi—not a cop.

Kyson nodded. That made sense. Flagging down a cop had thrown a monkey wrench into her plans. That answered the question why she hadn't wanted to file a report. The more he thought about it, the angrier he became. It wasn't often someone pulled the wool over his eyes. Perhaps if he'd been thinking with the right head last night, he would've seen through her shenanigans.

"Tough break, buddy," Griffin said, strolling up to Kyson's desk.

"Yeah," Kyson said, avoiding his ex-partner's gaze and slamming his top drawer shut.

Griffin sucked in a breath and rocked on his heels. "I tried to warn you she was a few cookies short of a dozen, didn't I?"

"Is that why you came over here? To tell me that you told me so?"

"Well, I did tell you so."

"I'm out of here," Kyson said, grabbing his small box of belongings.

"Whoa. Calm down. I'm sure the captain'll see the error of his ways. You'll be back on the job before you know it." Griff shrugged. "He's just blowing off steam. You know how he is."

"Sure. Whatever."

"He ripped you a new one, huh?"

"Something like that." Kyson turned away. "Take it easy, buddy," he said over his shoulder and gave a departing wave. He marched out of the precinct, avoiding eye contact. He knew without a doubt he would be the talk around the bar with the boys in blue. No need to give them more to laugh and gossip about.

Still, by the time he'd made it out to his car, he was certain he could chew through a box of nails. He needed answers and there was only one place to get them.

Michael marched into her house, throwing her keys on the foyer table and kicking her shoes clear into the living room. It wasn't enough to abate her anger. She was in serious trouble. This was nothing like the past, when she'd have overnight stints in jail for a minor misdemeanor. This was the big time.

She'd lied to the police. And there was a hundred percent chance she was going to get caught in that lie. But what could she do? Tell the truth and she would be hauled off to jail so fast her head would have spun. And not just her. Her foolish actions put her sisters at risk.

After all, hadn't Sheldon lied to the police, as well? And didn't Mike convince them to help put Phil into the trunk of her car and drive him across town? And what about Peyton? Michael had convinced her not to call the police—an accessory after the fact. The last thing she wanted was for P.J. to deliver her baby in jail. All in all, none of this sounded like the behavior of innocent women.

Oh what a tangled web we weave when first we practice to deceive.

"God, if you can get me out of this one, I swear from now on I'll be a good girl from here on out," she vowed, staring up at the ceiling.

BAM! BAM! BAM!

Michael nearly jumped ten feet since she was standing next to the door. Had they decided to come back and arrest her already? She hesitated, took a deep breath, and then wrenched open the door. This time there weren't two cops on the other side. Just one.

The one she didn't want to see.

"Kyson," she said thickly.

If looks could kill, Michael would have been

lying next to Phil in the morgue. "What are you doing here?" she asked.

"Surely you jest," he said, storming through the door without an invitation.

"I didn't say you could come in," she snapped.

"Sure you did. I heard you," he said, unfazed, cutting her a look that belied his words.

"Fine," she said, slamming the door behind him and then crossing her arms. "What do you want?"

"The truth," he said. "What else?" He turned away from her and stormed into the living room.

Michael took up the rear. "Hey! Where do you think you're going?"

"Going in to take a seat. You just offered me a seat, didn't you?"

"No. I didn't," she seethed. "Come back here," she barked. However, her words had no effect.

Kyson kept walking. He was heading for the basement door.

Michael panicked and raced around him to block his path. "I don't know what the hell you think you're doing," she snapped. "But you have exactly one minute to get out of here before I call the cops."

He cocked his head.

Oh, he was the police, she remembered.

How in the hell could she possibly forget? Reaching down, Michael turned the skeleton key jutting from the door, locking it. She then removed the key and dramatically slipped it into her bra.

Kyson's eyes followed the key's disappearance.

"Surely you don't think I won't go in after that."

"You wouldn't dare," she challenged.

"Wouldn't I?" His lips curled. "We're already familiar with each other in that area." He stepped forward. Just like that, the electricity that had always existed between them leaped off of him. "As a matter of fact, I don't think we finished where we left off this morning."

"Oh, we're definitely finished," she said.

Kyson lifted a lone brow that could have meant amusement, as well as curiosity. "So you're saying that I've served my purpose? Is that it?"

Michael frowned, unsure exactly what he meant. "C'mon, you know last night was just a...thing. Hell, we hardly know each other."

"You certainly got that right." He glared. "I thought I was making love to—"

"Making love?" she questioned.

Having sex is what he should have said, but it was too late.

Michael shook her head. "Look, I don't know what you thought but...well, you know, I'm just coming off a divorce and now he's—"

"Save it," he cut in. "I'm not interested. I used you and you used me. We both got what we wanted last night, right? Just a few hours of mind-blowing sex."

"Mind-blowing," she echoed.

Kyson rolled his eyes. "Look, I didn't come over

here to stroke your ego. I came here to get answers. Answers I think I'm entitled to."

"Look, I've already made my statement at the station. I have nothing further to add."

"What are you hiding downstairs?"

A chair. Rope. Duct tape. "Nothing," she lied.

"I didn't check it out for you last night. Maybe I should see if your so-called kidnappers are down there."

"That's not necessary."

"Uh-huh," he said, unconvinced. "Tell me, how's the rat problem coming along?"

Michael could feel the color drain from her face. "I'm handling it."

Kyson stared her down. In that instant he wanted to throttle her. How could he have been so blind? Sure, he thought she was a little eccentric, but a murderer? Was it truly possible?

"Last night, did you dump your ex-husband's body on Pacheco Pass?"

"Of course not!" Michael stomped her foot in indignation. "Now get the hell out of my house," she shouted.

"Why did you slash your tire last night?"

"What?"

"I saw that tire. That was no ordinary flat. Someone slashed the tire. I think it was you."

"And I think you've lost your mind."

"No. I finally found it. Granted, I was a little distracted last night." His eyes raked over her curvy figure. "I've got to hand it to you, that ripping-off-your-blouse thing was a good move. A damn good move. You needed me here as an alibi. But it's not going to work. Coroner says Matthews was killed at least seventy-two hours ago. Your plan has been shot to hell."

Michael had had enough. "Look, Detective Dekker. I'll say it one more time—I had nothing to do with my ex-husband's murder."

On cue, the phone rang.

She glanced across the room to stare at the cord-less by the sofa. She thought about answering it, but she didn't want to move away from the door. What if Kyson busted it down?

"Don't you think you should answer that?" Kyson asked after the second ring.

She held up her chin, uncertain of what to do.

Finally, the answering machine picked up. When she heard the voice coming on the machine, she almost fainted.

"Mikey, hey! It's your buddy, Ray Damon…"

Chapter 17

Michael nearly broke her neck racing to the phone. Never before had her living room seemed so wide or her limbs so heavy. By some miracle, she reached the answering machine before Ray Damon said anything that would implicate her in a possible murder.

"Hello, Ray!" she panted. "Hey! How are you?" She glanced over her shoulder to see Kyson staring at her as if she'd lost her mind.

"Mikey! Damn, girl. Scott and I have been glued to the news all morning. I can't believe it. You actually went through with it," he said, incredulous.

"What?" She swallowed, but the lump in her throat refused to budge. She tried to think while flashing an awkward smile at Kyson. "Um, I think there's been some kind misunderstanding," she said. Her eyes remained trained on the cop standing in her living room.

There was no doubt about it. Kyson had stopped being her one-night lover and transformed into a straightforward, no-nonsense police officer who, in all likelihood, would haul her butt into jail if given the chance.

"Man, Mike," Ray drawled. "I don't know about this." A note of worry seeped into his gruff voice. "When Scott and I agreed to help you out, we thought you were just going to scare the guy, you know. We never thought that you'd actually...*kill* him."

Michael closed her eyes and prayed for patience. Why did everyone think that she was capable of murder?

"But, um, Mikey. Me and my brother ain't cut out for this. Scottie already has a couple of strikes against him."

Why didn't they think about that before they kidnapped someone?

"I gotta tell ya," he continued. "You got us over here sweating bullets."

Try having a cop staring you in the face!

"Important call?" Kyson asked, moving toward her.

Michael stepped back and tried to unwedge the

lump in her throat a second time. "Ray, now is sort of a bad time for me. Can I call you back?" She hoped he'd take the hint.

"No. No. Now is a good time," he insisted. "We need to talk." He paused for a long exhalation. "What if the cops start snooping around and put two and two together? If you get caught then we get caught and that's just not cool."

Kyson took another step forward and Michael took another one back.

"There's bound to be fingerprints or something in that place. Scott and I weren't exactly careful that night. We had been drinking."

"You don't say," she responded drily.

"We need to get together so we all have our stories straight before the cops start popping up."

Too late, Michael thought. "Ray, really, this is not a good time." She searched around and found a pen. "Give me your number and I'll call you back."

"Mikey—"

"Ray," she cut him off. "I have company at the moment."

That shut him up for a moment. "You mean…?"

"Yes."

"Aw, man. Aw, man," he repeated, working himself up into a frenzy.

She waited for him to calm down while Kyson stalked her in a circle around the living room.

"All right," Ray said, finally pulling himself together. "I have one of those prepay cell phones, call me back on this number…"

Michael nodded and then proceeded to jot down the number across the palm of her hand. "Got it," she said and then quickly disconnected the call.

Kyson's stony expression remained in full effect. "Boy, you really have got men coming out of the woodwork."

Despite the somber look, Michael would have sworn she heard a note of jealousy. "Look, *Detective* Dekker, I've said all I have to say. Now I want you to leave."

Kyson leveled her with another long, hard stare. This time when he approached her, she held her ground. However, as he drew near, the molecules in the air shifted or changed. She suddenly felt light-headed and weak-kneed. What was it about this man that made her body commit mutiny against logic?

"I'll go," he said. "But now that you've dragged me into this mess, you better believe I'll be back." He stopped moving once his chest brushed against her heavy breasts.

When he looked down, Michael wondered whether he was considering reaching in for that damn key. She then wondered whether she had the strength or the desire to stop him.

Insanely, she craved his touch.

His caress.

His taste.

Had it been just this morning that they were lying in each other's arms, seemingly without a care in the world? It now felt like a lifetime ago.

What would it have been like had they met under different circumstances? Would he have stopped her on a street, in a mall or at a club? Would he have asked her for her phone number? Asked her out? What would their first date have been like?

She'd like to think they would've laughed the night away, shared stories or maybe even their dreams. One thing she was sure of, nothing would've changed in the bedroom or on top of the washing machine.

Michael finally swallowed that thick lump in her throat. She would never know how it could've been.

"I will find out what you're hiding," Kyson promised. "And when I do, believe me, I'll take great pleasure in being the one to put you in handcuffs this time."

She didn't mean to, but her legs had weakened a bit and she leaned into his chest. She was sure he hadn't meant for his words to be erotic, but it didn't stop the image of being handcuffed and submitting to his domination.

"Good day, Ms. Adams," he said.

The flash of desire she'd seen disappeared and he marched out of the living room and then out of the house. But he hadn't marched out of her life.

Not just yet.

* * *

"We're wasting time," the woman snapped. "Why don't we just go in there and grab her?"

"And what do you suppose we do about the cop?" the man growled back. "We have to wait for the right time."

"We don't *have* any more time. Our bosses are breathing down our necks. We need to deliver either the cash or the prototype pronto."

"I don't need you reminding me," he snapped, and then returned his attention down the street to see Detective Dekker walk out of Ms. Adams's house. "Good. Look, he's leaving."

"It's about time." The woman fidgeted while she looked up and down the neighborhood. "I hope these neighbors aren't as nosy as the ones in Matthews's neighborhood. Those old ladies police that area like armed prison guards." She sighed when Dekker climbed into his car. "You don't think Ms. Adams told the police about her ex-husband's illegal activities, do you?"

Her partner shrugged. "At this point anything is possible. That's why we need to be prepared."

She nodded, thought for a second. "There's also the chance she doesn't know anything. What are we going to do then?"

"She knows something. Why else would she have kidnapped him? She has to be in the game, too."

"But what if she doesn't know?"

He shrugged. "We'll cross that bridge when we come to it."

"Yeah. But if she doesn't know, what's to stop her from running to the police after we interrogate her?"

He laughed. "Trust me. When we're through with her she won't be talking to anyone else—ever again."

Chapter 18

It had been several minutes after Kyson had slammed the front door before Michael could manage to uproot herself from the center of the living room. She rushed to the front door and then glanced out the side panel of glass and watched as his car pulled out of the driveway.

Regret and indecision churned inside her. One thing for sure, she needed to do something. She didn't kill her husband and she could rule out the Damon twins, who were filling out some drunken contract hit as a favor. That meant there was a real killer on the loose.

Or killers.

Michael remembered the botched kidnapping

last night. Clearly they weren't a revenge team Phil had sent after her to even the score. Which meant…

They were *really* going to kill her last night. She glanced around, remembering the open door when she'd returned home and even the shadows in the bushes. They had been there.

But why?

The phone rang and Michael jumped—a habit she was developing. She raced back into the living room and snatched up the phone.

"Mikey," Sheldon exclaimed. The only way she knew it was Sheldon was by the number of babies screaming in the background. "Thank God you're back. What happened?"

"You don't want to know." Michael sighed. "It's gone from bad to worse."

"I didn't think that was possible."

Michael shook her head and thought for a moment. Didn't the bad guys always tap the phones in the movies—or was that the good guys? At this moment in her life everything seemed cast in gray. The bad guys wanted to kill her while the good ones wanted to lock her up and throw away the key.

Michael's gaze fell back to the number written across her hand. "Look, Sheldon, I have to go. I'll call you back."

"Call me back?" she thundered. "We need an emergency family meeting."

Michael laughed at that, as well. She was usually

the one who called family meetings. She had always been the ringleader—the one in control.

"Michael?" Sheldon prompted. "Are you still there?"

"Yeah." She sighed. "I'm here. Look, I'm going to have to call you back."

"Michael, this can't wait."

"I know." She glanced around again. She no longer felt safe in her own home. "I'm probably going to crash over at Dad's for a few days anyway."

"Yes, yes. Of course. Phil's death has hit us all pretty hard."

There was that, plus she was trying to avoid her own death, as well.

"Great, I'll let everyone know. By the way, Flex called, he's on his way here."

Michael smiled. Good ol' Flex. She may have been responsible for him running three thousand miles from home, but he could still be counted on whenever they needed him.

"Okay, I'll see everyone tonight," she said and rushed off the phone. Making a quick dash up the stairs, Michael threw clothes into an overnight bag. She would make good on her promise to stay at her father's, but first, she needed to see a set of twins.

Kyson wore out the punching bag before him. Sweat poured down his body and stung his eyes. He pounded the bag as if he was fighting a sworn enemy.

"Whoa, whoa. Ease up," Khail said, cutting in to hug the bag.

Kyson backed up, but still danced around ready for another round.

"C'mon, bro. You're overexerting. Pace yourself." Khail released the bag and Kyson rammed a quick dozen punches.

"Okay, okay," Khail cut in again. "Let's take five." He flung a towel around his brother's neck so he could mop his face.

Grudgingly, Kyson did what he was told while pulling in huge gulps of air.

Khail eyed his brother and then shook his head. "Whenever a man acts like this, it's got to be about a woman."

"Shut up. I'm not in the mood."

"Oh, yeah. It's definitely a woman. What did she do? Forget to tell you about her man? Run up your credit cards? Leave you for a woman?" Khail laughed at his own joke.

Kyson rolled his eyes and reached for his water bottle. He squirted a long stream into his mouth and then poured some over his head to cool off. He'd kept his training appointment, thinking it would be just the stress reliever he needed to get his mind right.

So far, it wasn't working.

The more he thought about Michael Adams, the more he felt like a fool. While it was true he liked his women on the wild side, suspected murderers were a definite no-no.

"All right. All right. This must be serious." Khail pulled him over to a nearby bench. "C'mon, tell your big bro what's up. Your mind obviously isn't on training, which means it's not on the pending fight. What did you do, break your celibacy rule?"

Kyson grunted.

"Thought so." Khail shook his head. "Hell, I guess getting laid is your kryptonite."

"Are you finished?"

Still chuckling, Khail tossed up his hands to indicate his surrender. "I'm all ears."

Exhaling a long breath, Kyson realized he didn't know where to begin. He leveled a look at his brother, debating. Finally, the need to confess to someone kicked in. "All right. There is this one woman."

"I knew it!" Khail slapped his knee.

"Can I please finish?"

"Sorry, sorry. My bad."

"I met this woman while investigating a missing person case. Anyway, there was something, a spark or something. I don't know." He shrugged. "I haven't felt anything like it since Jada, you know?"

Khail nodded.

"Well, my partner and I questioned this woman—nothing ever came of it. Anyway, our paths crossed again last night."

"Whoa." Khail stood. "Don't tell me this is about that fine brick house that came to our table last night."

"Look, you want to hear this story or not?" Kyson snapped.

"My bad. My bad. Go ahead."

"Well…" Hell, Kyson didn't know how to go into the last part. The alleged kidnappers, the supposed break-in, the pool—the sex. "Let's just say we *hooked up* last night," he spat.

Khail sat back down with a grin as wide as Texas. "Hooked up, huh? How was she?" He leaned in. "She was good, wasn't she? Probably all that and a bag of chips. I know. I can spot them a mile away."

"Oh, just forget it," Kyson said, jumping to his feet.

"Will you stop stalling and just tell me what the damn problem is," Khail said. "You hooked up, but you're acting as if… Wait. Did her husband walk in on you guys or something?"

"No." Kyson started walking back to the punching bag. His brother followed. "Let's just say that she's got herself into some trouble or she *is* trouble."

"Trouble how?"

Kyson made a weak swing at the punching bag. "The missing person case has now been upgraded to homicide."

Khail whistled low and then studied his younger

brother. "When you say a girl is trouble you don't be playing around, huh?"

Kyson sighed.

"You're not, uh, entangled in this, are you?" He shifted on his feet. "You weren't seduced into getting rid of an unwanted husband or some movie-of-the-week plot, were you?"

"No. But as of right now, I've been suspended from the department until further notice. Though now that you mention it, I hope that scenario you described isn't running through my captain's head."

"It didn't take me long to come up with it," Khail said.

Kyson cursed under his breath. Maybe that had been her aim, to pin Matthews's murder on him.

"Let me ask you," Khail said. "Do *you* think she's a murderer?"

Kyson was silent for a long time, remembering the passionate woman from last night—a woman who could still seduce him into bed even knowing what he knew now. Was he going crazy?

"I don't know," he answered, and then repeated Michael's words. "We hardly know each other."

"Then maybe you should find out."

He nodded. He planned on doing just that.

"Do you need any help?" Khail asked.

"Maybe," Kyson said. "I don't know if I can count on Griff to help me out on the DL. Not while my name is mud around the department."

"What do you need?"

"I need to find out everything I can on a Ray Damon."

Khail slapped Kyson on his sweaty back. "Consider it done, bro."

By the time Michael threw her bag into her car, she was clueless about the *sixteen* sets of eyes and three separate surveillance cars that followed her every move. Just barely peering above the steering wheel of a late-eighties model Cadillac sat Ms. Juanita Perkins and three of her geriatric cronies.

"Oh, this is so exciting," Louise said, clapping her hands behind Juanita's seat. "It's just like an episode of *Murder, She Wrote.*"

Two of the other ladies nodded in agreement while one frowned.

"I don't know about this," Beatrice spoke up. "I think we may be getting in over our heads with this one."

"Oh, don't chicken out on us now," Estelle snapped. "If Angela Lansbury can solve all those murders, surely we can solve one itsy-bitsy one."

Juanita nodded while Louise tried to adjust her wig for the umpteenth time.

Beatrice looked unconvinced. "I don't know."

"Oh, pooh, Beatrice," Juanita snapped. "Don't be an old fuddy-duddy. We already know who the murderer is, we just have to get information to prove it."

"But if she's truly a murderer, doesn't that make her dangerous? What are we going to do if we get caught—club her on the back of the head with our canes and sit on her until the cops come?"

"If need be," Juanita insisted. "I knew that girl was no good the moment I laid eyes on her. Just to think what she did to that sweet ex-husband of hers." Juanita drew a breath as if to prevent herself from getting too emotional. "Well, she simply won't get away with it."

Two heads nodded again in agreement while Beatrice hesitated.

"I know Michael was a bit of a rebel," Beatrice started, staring while the young lady pulled out of her driveway. "But a murderer? I'm sorry. I just don't see it."

"You're so naive, Beatrice," Juanita said, starting the car. "You never see the dark side of anyone. That's why every salesman is California has your number on speed dial."

Beatrice shrank in her seat, pouting.

"Okay, we better get going," Estelle said. "She's pulling off."

"I'm going. I'm going." Juanita pulled away from the curb. "One of you should've reminded me to bring my glasses."

In an unmarked police car down the street, Detective Griffin squinted at the carful of old ladies as they whipped past him. "Is that...?" He frowned, thought about it and then shook his head. "It couldn't have been…then again…"

"What?" Detective Martinez asked.

"That car that just passed…"

"Yeah, what about it?" Martinez asked as she pulled away from the curb.

"I think I know them."

"Oh?"

"Yeah, I could almost swear they were the neighborhood watchdogs over at Philip Matthews's place."

Martinez laughed. "You're kidding."

Griff shook his head. "This case keeps getting stranger by the minute."

Chapter 19

Michael had made it as far as Mathilda Avenue in Sunnyvale before she'd spotted a black SUV in her rearview mirror. She tried to reason that there was no need to panic—after all, there were thousands of Ford Explorers on the roads—but she wondered just how many had a pair of blue fuzzy dice hanging from the rearview mirror.

Was there a pair of blue dice in the SUV from last night? She couldn't remember. Besides, it was dark. She didn't see much.

But it was possible.

"Okay, Mike," she whispered. "Don't panic. Stay calm." She made an impromptu right turn on the next available street and then watched the rearview to see whether the SUV would make an appearance.

It did.

Michael's grip tightened on the steering wheel. "Oh my God. Oh my God. It's them." Heart racing, she struggled to maintain her car lane. "Think. Think."

While her mind raced, her stomach clenched into a tight knot. "Look for the police," came her only answer. She groaned and rolled her eyes. Maybe that wasn't such a hot idea. Whoever these people were, they would undoubtedly disappear into thin air again, leaving her to look like an hysterical loony the way she did last night.

Michael took another right, then left, and right again. When the SUV remained hot on her tail, Michael did the only thing she could think of: put the pedal to the metal and burned rubber. After all, she grew up on *Smokey and the Bandit* movies and once was the queen of the go-carts when she was a kid. Surely that qualified her to shake an unwanted tail.

Car horns blared as she darted in and cut people off as she tried to fight her way back to the main highway. She would have to meet the Damon twins another time. The last thing she wanted was to lead potential trouble…or rather *more* trouble to their doorstep.

Right now she needed to get somewhere safe.

"What on earth is that child doin'?" Juanita asked, struggling to keep up. By Michael's third turn, the

Neighborhood Watch girls tossed in the towel. "Didn't I tell you that girl was a menace to society?"

Louise tsked behind her. "She going to kill somebody else out here, driving like a maniac."

Juanita pulled over to the side of the road. Her slow reflexes and weakened eyesight was no match against her former next-door neighbor.

"There's got to be a better way to do this," Estelle stressed.

"I agree," said Louise. "I don't think my heart can stand another trip like this one. We need to fall back and regroup—devise a better plan in goin' about this thing."

Juanita grudgingly agreed and then slowly turned the long car around in order to take them home. "We'll get her. Mark my words. We'll get her."

"I think she's spotted us," Martinez complained, trying to keep up with Michael's erratic driving. It worked for a few blocks, but the streets were crowded and she had no real reason to give chase. "I wonder how she spotted us."

"Maybe it's not us she spotted," Griff grumbled, thinking of the old ladies but then spotting a black SUV. "Now, who is this?" he grumbled, angling to take a closer look. "Can you get a fix on the tags of that Ford Explorer?" he asked his new partner.

"What?" Martinez asked, distracted.

Griff leaned closer toward the dashboard, trying

to make out the license plate himself. No doubt about it, the Ford Explorer remained locked on Ms. Adams's tail. "This lady has more people following her than a marching band in the Macy's Thanksgiving Day parade."

"Oh, I see them," Martinez said, spotting the SUV. "Who do you think it is?"

"At this point, I wouldn't be surprised if it was the CIA," he grumbled, finally catching a good glimpse of the tag and jotting it down.

Martinez maintained her tail for two more blocks and then cursed when both the SUV and the Volvo lost her on Highway 680. "I don't believe this." She tossed up her hands. "Where in the hell did these people learn to drive?"

"Don't worry about it," Griff said. "She'll pop up again. Let's go back to the station. Something just doesn't feel right about all this."

Chapter 20

"Where on earth is she?" Frankie asked, moving away from the window and pacing around the family table. "She should've been here hours ago."

Joey and Peyton hung their heads and stared at the mahogany table in collective misery.

"Something has to be wrong," Peyton said.

"Isn't it always when it comes to Michael?" Joey countered.

Hearing footsteps on the staircase, the girls looked up and waited until Sheldon and Donna rejoined them at the table.

"Kids are asleep?" Frankie asked.

Sheldon had brought her two youngest and Donna had, of course, put Teddy to bed.

"They're out like a light," Donna said, folding her arms and leaning against the dining-room door frame. "Any word yet?"

The three sisters shook their heads.

"This is not a good sign," Sheldon said, joining her sisters at the table. "Can this day possibly get any worse?"

No one answered. With Michael, it could always get worse.

"So what do you girls think?" Donna asked. "Is it really possible Michael could've had something to do with Phil's death?"

"I'm trying not to go there," Peyton said, rubbing her belly and adjusting in her chair.

Joey sighed. "I can't imagine Michael willingly having anything to do with killing Phil. I mean, she just wouldn't. We all know Michael's bark is worse than her bite."

The sisters nodded in agreement.

"Michael wouldn't hurt a fly," she added. "Not intentionally, anyway."

Sheldon sat down, as well.

"But what about those Damon twins you girls were talking about?" Donna asked. "Do you think they could've done this?"

The girls darted glances at one another.

Peyton drew a deep breath since she, more than the other girls, had firsthand experience with the Damon twins. After all, they and her first husband, Ricky, had been best friends.

At one time the Damon twins had been a constant fixture in her home. They, like her first husband, harbored dreams of breaking into the music industry. Also like her ex-husband, they lacked the talent.

As far as Peyton knew, they were hustlers by trade and dreamers by hobby. Ray Damon's few stints in jail never amounted to anything serious. Scott was another story.

The twins had a special knack for finding trouble or trouble had a knack for finding them—whatever the case might be. The two of them plus Michael could only equal bad news.

A pair of headlights pierced the window. The women jumped to their feet, including the very large and pregnant Peyton, and nearly bowled each other over trying to get to the window to see who had arrived.

"Is it her?" Frankie asked from the back of the cloister.

After making out the silver Lexus sedan, four sets of shoulders slumped in disappointment, but then lifted when they remembered the men were returning home from the airport with their baby brother, Flex.

They all rushed to the front door; this time, Peyton brought up the rear.

"Flex!" they shouted, throwing the door open and racing outside.

The result was a big group hug while Flex's boisterous laugh fell over them. "Now this is what I call a homecoming!" Flex said and then allowed them to pull him into the house.

A series of ahs and ohs floated around him as his sisters took in his recent thirty-five-pound weight loss. Though he had always been a big guy, the last time they had seen him he had packed on a few unwanted pounds, which was a job hazard for a firefighter.

Since his move to Decatur, Georgia, Flex's career had only flourished. He had been hailed a hero several times in the local newspaper. The first time was when he'd saved Linc's life. They became fast friends, but Flex had lied to his family and said that he was actually dating his now brother-in-law. Meanwhile, Linc and Peyton met and were secretly dating behind his back. It had been a humorous train wreck when the lies collided.

At long last the hugs loosened and Flex glanced around. "Where's Michael?"

The smiles faded instantly.

"She hasn't made it here yet?" Marlin asked, his own worry lines creasing his forehead.

"No," Donna said, sliding an arm around her husband. "She hasn't called, either."

Linc and Ryan took their positions next to their wives to offer their comfort, as well.

"Have you tried calling her?" Ryan asked, squeezing Joey tight. "Maybe she's still at her house."

"We've been calling every five minutes," she said. "She's not answering any of her phones."

The men's reactions now matched the women's.

"Maybe she just changed her mind about coming," Flex said.

But that didn't feel right to any of them.

"Why don't we go into the living room," Flex said. "Everyone can fill me in on what's really going on."

"I'll go get the bottle of Excedrin," Sheldon said. When Flex frowned, she added, "Trust me. You're going to need it."

K.D. Dekker Investigative Services was one of two business still renting in an old run-down strip mall off Ponds Avenue. The other stores and businesses had left long ago for more fancy, profitable buildings near Santana Row. Khail liked the location because the lease was cheap and there was always plenty of parking.

For the most part, he kept late hours. Mainly because most of his clients were interested in domestic snooping, where one spouse suspected the other of cheating. This usually required him being camped out in a nondescript car outside an equally nondescript motel most nights—too many nights.

That said, he didn't mind being in his office late doing his baby brother a favor.

"You got lucky," Khail said.

Kyson stood hunched over his brother's shoulder, reading the computer screen.

"There are not that many R. Damons in the San Jose area. The only Ray I see has a current address in Sunnyvale."

"Is that him?" Kyson asked, indicating the picture of a very light-skinned brother with obvious Puerto Rican features.

"Yep," Khail confirmed. "That's Ray 'Pretty Boy' Damon. I guess that means he's popular with the ladies…or fellas," he added for a chuckle.

Jealousy pricked Kyson's pride as he evaluated the man. Until this moment, he hadn't given much thought to Ray Damon's possibly intimate relationship with Michael. "He's all right."

Khail glanced over his shoulder, laughed.

"What?" Kyson asked.

Khail shook his head. "If you don't know, I'm not saying."

Ignoring him, Kyson asked, "What was he in for?"

"Couple of DUIs, one breaking and entering and, this is interesting, carrying a weapon without a license." Khail scrolled through the pages. "It says here he pistol-whipped some guy in a club back in '91 for grabbing his woman's butt. Oh…" He leaned back in his chair.

"What?" Kyson asked.

"Check out the named woman."

He leaned forward, his eyes snagged the line. "Ms. Michael Anthony Adams."

"Looks like he and your girl go way back."

Kyson clenched his jaw as jealousy spread through his system like a virus.

Khail fiddled with the computer some more and clicked around a few links. "Well, lookie here." Another image popped onto the screen. "Looks like your boy is a twin."

"What?"

"Scott Damon," Khail read. "Now, this brother here has a rap sheet a mile long." He scrolled through the list. "I gotta tell ya. It ain't looking too good for your girl. If she's friends with men like these…"

Even though his brother didn't finish the sentence, Kyson knew what was left unsaid. "Thanks for your help, bro," he muttered, struggling to rein in his temper.

"Not a problem." Khail turned in his chair. "Glad I could help."

Kyson nodded, walked away from the desk and headed toward the door.

"Are you going to be all right?"

He stopped before the door. "You know me. I take a lickin' and keep on tickin'."

Khail studied him. His usual jovial demeanor was gone. "Look, I know it's been awhile since you've taken advice from your older brother, but maybe this time you might consider humoring me."

Kyson remained quiet.

"I know you like her, but if I were you I'd run the other way from this chick. Trouble doesn't describe this. This is bad news. We're talking life-changing bad news. Let this one go."

He nodded. "Thanks again."

"Don't mention it."

Kyson escaped his brother's office and stormed toward his car. The more he thought about it, the more he became convinced that Michael Adams was nothing more than a lying, scheming, conniving woman who had played him.

He jerked open his car door and then slammed it once he was inside, but before he could place the key into the ignition, his cell phone rang.

"Yeah," he answered.

"Kyson?" Michael's voice trembled on the line. "Kyson, I need your help."

Chapter 21

Michael had never been so scared in all her life. How could a day that had started so beautifully have ended so badly? It had been hours since she'd shaken the tail of the mysterious black SUV. At least this time she had gotten a good glimpse of the driver: a tall, mahogany brother whose bulky muscles seemed to have their own muscles. It was a wonder that she had ever gotten away from him last night.

She couldn't make out much more since he wore black shades and black clothing. One thing for sure, he looked like one mean son of a bitch.

In the passenger seat, Michael nearly had to do

a double take. There sat the driver's polar opposite: a short, petite Asian woman in the same black shades, clothes, and even the same evil look.

Who were these people? And what in the hell did they want? The two questions tumbled through her mind until fresh tears surfaced.

On Highway 101, Michael had made it as far as San Francisco before Detective Griffin's warning had filtered back into her fear-riddled brain. Even though jail seemed like a better choice than death, Michael turned around, suddenly certain that there was only one man who could help her.

Of course there was a vast difference between someone being able to help and someone *willing* to help. Remembering how she and Kyson had separated hours ago, there was a very good chance Kyson would turn her away.

First, Michael thought it would be best if she ditched her car. Since her modern-day Bonnie and Clyde had a fix on her vehicle, she needed to become a little more incognito, and fast.

She had thought about calling one of her sisters to come and meet her—was even seconds from dialing the number when it occurred to her that she'd be putting members of her family at risk. Maybe it was best to lay low until she could figure this whole thing out.

Figuring that it was best to blend into a large crowd, Michael parked her Volvo at the Great Mall and then decided to huff her way to the Blue Note Lounge, a small hole-in-the-wall bar a mile up from the mall.

Being out in the open increased Michael's paranoia. If she truly hadn't lost her tail, she was a sitting duck. Every five seconds she glanced over her shoulder and froze up whenever a black SUV drove down the street.

By the time she reached the Blue Note, she was an emotional wreck. There was nothing impressive about the bar. Its size was roughly the same as her father's living room. At least it was dark, reasonably crowded and it had a bar.

"Evening! What can I getcha?" the bartender, a middle-aged African-American woman with a crayon-yellow buzz cut, inquired.

"The strongest you got," Michael said, working her way onto a bar stool and glancing around.

On the dance floor, if you wanted to call it that, two drunks struggled to keep in time with Kanye West's latest hit. At one table a group of four friends laughed and pointed at the television screen above one corner of the bar.

The rest of the Blue Note's patrons lined the bar, hunched over on old stools and nursing their drinks. A few guys were playing dice and exchanging dollars back and forth as if they were high rollers in Vegas.

Michael's drink arrived in record time and she tossed the contents back like it was water. She winced through the alcohol's burn and barked, "Another."

"You got it," the bartender said and quickly refilled her glass.

This time Michael downed the contents slower. She was grateful. She was grateful for how quickly the liquor stilled her nerves. "Hey, do you have a phone around here?" she asked, disappointed that she'd left her cell phone hooked up to her car's charger.

"Over there by the bathrooms," the bartender instructed.

"Okay. Thanks." She slapped twenty dollars on the bar and stood. The fact that there was a pay phone said a lot about the place.

She had no trouble finding the business card Kyson had given her on the first day they'd met. On the back was his cell phone number. Michael quickly shoved quarters into the phone. When he answered, her stomach looped into crazy knots.

"Kyson," she said, voice trembling. "Kyson, I need your help."

A long silence followed.

Fearful he'd hung up, she tried again. "Kyson, are you there?"

"Yeah. Where are you?"

"I'm at a place called the Blue Note Lounge. It's a bar off Capitol. Do you know where that is?"

Silence.

"Kyson, please. I'm really in trouble and I don't know who else to call."

"You could always call your buddy, Ray Damon."

"What?" she thundered incredulously. Had the police already found out about her and the twins? Then she remembered him being at her place when Ray called. "Kyson, it's not what you think. Trust me."

This time she heard his long exhalation.

"All right. Stay put. I'm on my way."

"Thank you," she said at the same time there was a click. He hung up. As she returned the receiver back to its cradle, a part of her was relieved.

Michael returned to the bar and reviewed whether she'd made the right decision. There was not much to review; it was either him or call the twins. Common sense told her when one was running from trouble not to run toward *more* trouble.

"Can I get you anything else?"

"Yeah. I'll have another of the same."

"You got it, honey."

When the third drink was set down, Michael took her time nursing it, waiting. She didn't have to wait long.

Fifteen minutes later, Kyson entered the small lounge and immediately locked gazes with her at the bar. Michael fluttered a relieved smile. But one look at his iron face, and she was reminded to keep her emotions in check.

Just as Kyson approached the bar, the man sitting

next to her paid his tab and left. Kyson took the empty stool next to Michael. "All right. I'm here," he said evenly. "What's your game?"

Michael hopped off her stool. "Are you parked outside?"

"Whoa. Whoa. Slow your horses." He patted her vacant stool. "Sit. Let's talk."

She ignored the order. "We'll talk in the car."

"I'm not sure I like that idea," he countered.

Michael moved in close so that her words could fall into his ears only. "It's not safe to talk here." She glanced around. "Anyone could be listening."

Kyson studied her for a long moment and then started chuckling. "I gotta hand it to you. You're one fine piece of work. You have a sister in the movie biz, right? Maybe you should hit her up for an acting gig."

Michael straightened her spine and lifted her chin at the quick barb. The action also caused her breasts to rise proudly, and Kyson's eyes followed the moment carefully.

"Did you come here to help me or not?"

"That depends," he said lazily.

"On what?"

"On what you need help with." He stared back. "Any more dead bodies you need to unload?"

Michael stepped back. A sudden surge of tears burned the back of her eyes. "Forget it. I made a mistake."

After slinging her large bag over her shoulder,

she moved to step from the bar. She didn't need him. She didn't need anybody. Her world was crumbling around her and he was acting as if she had just escaped from a mental institution.

She was, however, on the verge of a nervous breakdown and couldn't do a damn thing about it.

Kyson's hand shot out, captured her wrist and dragged her back. At the sight of her burgeoning hysteria, Kyson loosened his grip and his heart-strings yielded. If she was an actress, she was a damn good one.

"Let go of me," she commanded. "I'm sure I've wasted enough of your time."

"All right. All right," he said, standing. "We'll play this thing your way. You need a ride out of here so we can talk—fine. I'll take you. Where do you want to go?"

Michael looked up through shimmering tears and said, "Take me to your place."

Chapter 22

No ifs, ands or buts about it, Kyson needed to get his head examined. One look into her glossy eyes, hearing her desperate plea, he'd dragged her out of the Blue Note so fast, she'd had trouble keeping up with him. If she wanted to go to his place, then fine, he'd take her there. The game now was to see whether she really wanted to talk or whether she had other things on her mind.

If it was *other things,* would he have the strength to reject her?

Kyson pushed that question to the back of his mind. He jerked opened the passenger door and held it open for her to climb inside.

Michael bypassed his offer for the backdoor.

"What are you doing?" he asked, suspicious.

"I think I'd better hide in the back," she said. She made a quick glance around the sparse parking lot.

"Hide?" He watched as she struggled to hunker down on the back floorboard behind the passenger seat.

"Hey, can you help move the seat up for me?" she asked.

Frowning, Kyson did as asked and pulled the passenger seat closer to the dashboard.

Once she'd squeezed into the tight space, she mumbled a thanks.

"You're welcome," he said, shaking his head and closing both doors. As he walked to the other side, he couldn't help thinking this entire episode should be captured on the old TV show *Candid Camera*.

Quickly, he climbed into the driver's seat and started the car. For the first few minutes, silence crackled in the small compartment. What did one say in a situation like this?

It was nearing midnight. They were tired and wired at the same time.

"I didn't kill my ex-husband," she said suddenly.

Kyson glanced back but said nothing.

"I know you don't believe me," she added, her voice thick with emotion. "But I think I know who did it."

Kyson's grip tightened on the steering wheel.

Was this the part when she'd blame her two cohorts, claim they did it on their own accord or admit that she was caught up in some weird love triangle?

He waited in anxious anticipation, mentally urging her to continue. Instead what he received was tears. Not the long dramatic weepy kind of a seasoned actress, but the silent, heart-wrenching kind that softened his heart against his will.

"I know that I was angry with him, but I truly, truly didn't want anything bad to happen." She sniffed. "Phil and I had been together for ten years. We were friends once—a long time ago. He was a prankster…sort of like me. We came from opposite sides of the tracks. He always thought that he had something to prove.

"Phil used to tease me that my family was like the Huxtables. He believed that money was never an issue. I could never convince him that wasn't true. People always want to believe that the grass is greener on the other side."

Michael fell silent for a while and then continued. "We lost my mom to cancer. Dad struggled to keep everything together, but…anyway, I saw how everyone was falling apart. I stepped up—sort of planted myself as the mother hen of the family. Maybe sometimes I overdid it, but with a family of seven—it wasn't easy." She mopped at her face. "I told Phil this, but he only saw what he wanted to see. He used to share his story about how he'd struggled to put himself through college. He thought of himself as a hustler, robbing Peter to pay Paul most of his life. I didn't see it at first. But Phil was always desperate for success. He wanted more than what he grew up with."

"Who doesn't?" Kyson cut in softly.

"Yeah. I thought so, too," she said. "Then Frankie married a millionaire, Joey an insanely rich Hollywood director. While I know we were both happy for them, it seemed to raise the bar for Phil. He wanted to be as successful as his brothers-in-law.

"All he talked about was making more and more money. Nothing was ever good enough. I never cared what he had...or what he didn't have for that matter, I just wanted to be married." She emitted a sad little laugh. "I don't think I really cared who it was, I just wanted the title of Mrs. So-and-So so much that I overlooked a lot of things—too many things."

"Why?" Kyson asked, drawn into the story.

"Every woman wants to be married," she said. "We all want to *belong* to someone even if we don't realize it."

The car fell silent again while Kyson realized it was true for men, too, but he figured out long ago that it was more important to belong to the *right* somebody. He glanced back. Maybe she was just figuring that out, as well.

"Anyway," she finally said. "That was our marriage. Pathetic, huh?"

He weighed his answer. "I've heard worse," he admitted.

"Yeah, well. Phil and I dated a few years, we were engaged even longer. The sad part was that our marriage was over almost as soon as it began. Phil worked most of the time and was never really around. He was always angling to get ahead, trying to make the big score. I was ready for the next step."

"Kids?" he asked.

"First comes love, then comes marriage. It was time for the baby carriages." Michael drew a deep breath. Her voice had finally grown stronger. "Phil kept saying that he wanted to wait until we were financially ready. As far as I could tell, we were. He made good money, but it was not enough for him. That started the fighting."

Michael quieted while Kyson continued driving, eyes straight ahead.

"Phil wasn't a bad man," she said in conclusion. "He was just the wrong man for me. The wrong man at the right time."

Kyson didn't know what to make of Michael's long soliloquy, but he had plenty of time to run it through his mind a few times before he reached his gated apartment complex. He punched in his security code and eased down to his designated parking spot.

"Are we there?" she asked.

"We're here. Home sweet home," he said, shutting off the engine. He exhaled a long breath and then asked himself one last time whether he wanted to do this. When no answer came, he went ahead and climbed out of the car.

He walked around the vehicle, opened the back door and helped her out. Only the sound of their shoes slapping the pavement broke the night's silence. After he unlocked his door, he held it open and waited.

Michael took a deep breath and crossed the threshold. She inched inside like a scared rabbit.

Kyson flipped on the light switch and bathed the apartment in light. "Make yourself at home." He removed his jacket and hung it on a peg by the door.

She set down her bag and did likewise. "Thank you," she whispered and turned back to access his sparsely decorated apartment. "Nice place," she said, awkwardly following him into the living room, taking her bag.

"Thanks," he said. "Can I get you something to drink?"

"Water, if you don't mind."

"Bottled or filtered?"

"Bottled."

"Coming right up." Kyson headed to the kitchen.

Michael set her bag next to the coffee table, still feeling awkward in her new surroundings.

Returning quickly, Kyson handed over the bottled water. "Here you go."

"Thanks."

"Don't mention it." He glanced around. "Won't you have a seat?"

She nodded and settled into a plush, earth-toned sofa. "So how long have you lived here?"

"Why don't you tell me who killed your ex-husband?"

Their questions had overlapped one another and Kyson had the unpleasantness of watching her tears resurface.

"You're not going to believe me," she said, dropping her gaze to the label of her bottled water.

"None of that has mattered so far," he said, determined not to be swayed by tears a second time.

Michael drew a couple of shaky breaths and then downed half the bottled water.

Kyson watched her wearily as she placed the bottle on the coffee table and then folded her hands into her lap.

"I don't know who they are," she said.

"That's not what you said in the car."

Annoyance flashed in her eyes. "What I meant was I don't know their names."

"Uh-huh."

"But they've been following me. Today they chased me all over town. It's the same SUV that pulled behind my car last night."

"The kidnappers?" he asked for clarification.

She nodded.

Kyson rolled his eyes. He couldn't help it. "Look, Mike—"

"I'm telling you the truth!"

"Is that right?" he thundered back, equally annoyed. "The truth? Why don't we start this over and you tell me exactly what you're hiding in your basement."

"What? My basement?"

"Yes! Why wouldn't you let me go downstairs?"

Michael jumped to her feet. "Will you forget about the damn basement? I'm trying to tell you that I know who killed my ex-husband—people who are trying to kill me!"

"They're trying to kill you now? I thought that they just wanted to kidnap you."

"They did! They do!"

Kyson also jumped to his feet. "Get your story straight. Do these people merely want to kidnap you or do they want to kill you?"

"I don't know what they want," she shouted, her hysteria returning in full force.

"C'mon, Mike. Something's not adding up. If someone was truly trying to kidnap or kill you last night, why didn't you want to report it? Why wouldn't you file a report? Why wouldn't you file a description of these so-called kidnappers?"

"Because I, uh…"

"Hmm? I can't hear you."

Because I thought my husband was paying me back for kidnapping him. "Just because! All right?"

"Just because," he repeated. "Well, that's certainly different."

Michael groaned.

"You know, I would have thought a dramatic actress like yourself would have come up with a better reason than that."

"I'm not acting!"

"But you're not telling the whole truth, either."

She fell silent.

"Oh, come on. Everything about you is a big act. Last night was a big act—the slashed tires, disappearing kidnappers, alleged break-ins with nothing stolen, and let's not forget the big seduction number to get me to be your damn alibi when my cop buddies came sniffing around."

She gasped. "I didn't make love to you for a damn alibi."

"Oh, it's making love now?"

"I didn't have *sex* with you for an alibi."

"Well?" He moved in close. "Why did you do it?"

"Because I…because I thought…because I felt…"

"You felt what?" he challenged, pressing his chest into hers. "You felt what?"

She sputtered again, the English language a fading memory.

"Maybe I should show you what I felt," he said hoarsely, grabbing her by the waist and crashing his lips against hers.

Chapter 23

Michael's body exploded with immeasurable pleasure while her mind careened into the heavens. God, how could she have forgotten it was like this with him? She moaned while his silken tongue glided over hers, sighed when his strong hands cupped and squeezed her breasts and trembled when his sex pressed against the softness of her belly.

They were both on fire.

Their clothes flew off in just a few blinks. Naked, Kyson and Michael tumbled to the floor, their bodies snapped together like a puzzle, both caught in the need to be together.

Kyson thought he was hard until his hand

brushed against the velvet curls guarding the moist pink cavern between her legs. Now he was on the verge of exploding. He'd wanted to avoid this. It was why he had held on to his anger, but nothing had prepared him for this wonderful tide of emotion.

Michael Adams may be trouble; she may even be bad news. But right now in this moment in time, she belonged to him.

And if he had his way, he would never let her go.

Kyson lifted himself up during her soft whimpering moans and glided his fingers inside her moist entrance. Back and forth he probed while his mouth slanted across hers.

The sound of their breathing—his raspy, hers shallow—fell in tune with the pounding of their hearts.

Michael caressed his arms, his shoulders and his back while her hips surged forward in time with his fingers' wondrous strokes. It wasn't long before she shivered with pleasure, alerting him that her first orgasm was just seconds away.

Kyson's hot mouth abandoned hers to slide down her chin, neck and over to a bountiful breast.

Michael's head lolled, her eyes closed as she rode a wave of pleasure. Her uninhibited response to his touch served as a visual aphrodisiac.

Kyson's hand shook and the ache of his sex became painful.

Michael's sighs became a gasping falsetto while stars flashed behind her closed lids as her first orgasm eclipsed. Weak, light-headed, Michael's heart pounded a thunderous beat.

Kyson magically produced a condom and slid it on. He wasted no time entering her. The moment their bodies met, he nearly lost control. It had been the same way with her the first time. He loved her body's softness and he found that he wanted to touch her everywhere, pound his way into her heart.

Michael felt like a melted pool of wax. So loose, so languid. The feel of him inside of her was overwhelming. He was so hard. So hot. So big.

How was it that he was able to swallow her up? How did he make her burn so bright and not become a pile of cinders as their hips rocked, her breasts rubbing against his chest, flaring heat into her rock-hard nipples?

When her moans climbed, Kyson brushed small kisses along her jaw, nose and then finally slanted back across her mouth. The kiss was hot, wet and overwhelmingly erotic. He gave his tongue, she caught it between her teeth, teased him.

Kyson growled low.

Michael arched against him, taking him deeper. Just when she was about to come, he pulled back and commanded her to, "Get on your knees."

She rushed to do what she was told, then gasped again in pleasure when he entered her from behind.

"Oh, baby. Yes!" Kyson kissed her back.

Michael slid her arms across the carpet, perking her butt higher in the air. She wanted desperately to feel every inch of him and was pleased that he was determined to give her what she wanted.

A sheen of perspiration covered Kyson's brow.

Michael felt hot, wet and wonderful all over. In no time, he'd flipped her back over, reclaimed her mouth and continued to hammer away while their tongues found their own mating dance.

She whimpered, trembled and quaked as her body yielded to her next orgasm.

"That's it, baby. That's it," he coached, slipping his thumb between her feminine folds to caress her clit.

Her climax shot off like a rocket.

Almost immediately, Kyson's did the same.

Exhausted, the lovers collapsed and lay panting on the floor.

The reality of what they'd just done slowly seeped into their consciousness. When it did, Kyson was the first to chuckle and then start laughing.

Still struggling to catch her breath, Michael glanced at him, almost too afraid to ask, "What's so funny?"

"We are," he confessed. "Don't tell me that you, of all people, don't see the humor in all this."

"Actually, I don't." She turned away. "I didn't call you so you could bring me here and seduce me."

"Seduce you? Lady, I like your nerve." He sat up and glanced down at her. However, that was a big mistake. One look at her luscious body and he was hard all over again.

Unaware of his sudden lustful thoughts, Michael sat up, as well, and looked around for her clothing. "Look, I'm tired of this. It's obvious you don't believe me and don't want to help me." She found a shirt and shoved it on. "Where's your bathroom so I can take a shower? Then I'll get out of your hair for good."

Standing, her full apple bottom moved before his face.

Kyson went temporarily deaf as his gaze locked on her lovely behind.

Michael looked over, catching his stare. How could a woman not be flattered? She cleared her throat and broke his lustful trance.

"Upstairs." Her question finally sank in. "The shower is through the master bedroom."

"Thanks," she said, turning toward the staircase. She was halfway up when she felt his hand on her wrist. She stopped, turned.

"When you come out, I think we need to discuss your going to the station tomorrow morning to file a report—that's if what you're saying is true. You need to get everything on record."

"I'd rather you help me find out who these people chasing me around town are."

"That is the job of the police."

Michael shook her head. "No offense, but me and the police don't mix."

"I thought we mixed rather well."

Her face flushed while she held his stare. For a few long seconds, she wavered on what to do. Telling the whole truth would mean admitting that she'd lied about her husband's disappearance, the kidnapping—everything. "How about I promise to think about it?"

Kyson cocked his head. "You'll think about it?"

"Yes," she said. "That's all I can promise for right now."

He spat out a disbelieving chuckle. "C'mon. What's your pl— What is it that you really want me to do? Why did you call me?"

She sighed. "Just help me find out who they are and what they want."

Disappointment shone clearly in his expression.

She waited for his answer. When it didn't seem as if one was forthcoming, she probed, "Well?"

"How about I'll think about it?"

Michael lifted her chin. "Fair enough." She held his gaze and leaned forward and kissed him, softly at first, but, loving the taste, she pressed harder and ignited a fire she couldn't contain.

Kyson moaned like a man being tortured.

Immediately drunk with power, she stepped down one stair as their bodies brushed together while she wrapped a hand around his swollen sex.

He sucked in a breath, drawing her bottom lip in between his teeth.

It didn't matter. She was too caught up, sliding her hands along his silky shaft. She loved the feel of him.

She took two steps down so that now he towered above her. Then she slowly sank to her knees while maintaining eye contact.

Kyson's eyes widened as she gently kissed the tip of his shaft and then boldly flicked her tongue against the head. His flesh became hard as steel as she unabashedly slid it between her lips.

"Sweet Jesus," he moaned.

That was her thought exactly. His tangy sweetness was the most delicious thing she'd ever had and she was determined to have as much of him and for as long as she wanted.

Kyson lacked the ability to remain standing. He slowly lowered himself to sit on a stair; it was either that or tumble down. Regardless, Michael's mouth never broke contact during her wondrous sucking. Jointly, her warm mouth, tight throat and silky tongue had to be the eighth wonder of the world.

He could almost swear that she was trying to suck the soul out of him. He leaned back, spread his legs wide and watched her work her magic. All the while, she never took her eyes off of him.

"Oh God," he recited, tangling his hands in her hair. Her teasing brought him to the brink a few times, but then she slowed her rhythm to prolong his pleasure.

Kyson tried to cheat by lifting his hips and

pumping a few extra strokes. Finally she hit the magic spot, caused his eyes to roll into the back of his head as he unleashed a mother lode.

When his breathing returned to normal, he saw the wicked grin on her face and had the sudden urge to pay her back.

"Your turn," he said, making her crawl up on all fours the length of his body until the apex of her sex hovered above his open mouth. He then proceeded to polish the pink pearl between her legs with long, smooth strokes of his tongue.

Michael's pleasure-filled moans echoed throughout the apartment, making him hard again. He slipped one hand into her wet body and kept the other locked around his shaft; both pumped away while his tongue drove her toward madness.

In no time, she was trying to crawl away from the intense pleasure but, in the end, she was too weak to get too far.

"Don't think I'm finished with you yet," he said, sliding from beneath her only to pop back up and enter her from behind.

Michael grabbed hold of the banister while Kyson rocked her body in a violent storm of thrusts.

It was all too much.

Too consuming.

Too wonderful.

When her body exploded, she swore she nearly blacked out from the overwhelming sensations.

A few strokes later, Kyson roared and sent a hot spray of semen against her back and then collapsed beside her on the stairs.

At some point, somehow they made it to his bedroom, took their showers and then passed out as soon as their bodies fell onto the bed. However, Michael had not planned on waking up—handcuffed.

Chapter 24

"Good morning, sunshine." Kyson smiled above her. "Sleep well?"

Michael pulled at her hands, dismayed to find that not only were her hands cuffed, but her feet had been cuffed to the foot of the bed, as well. "What is going on?"

Kyson's smile turned wicked. "Well, I figured that turnabout is fair play." He winked. "Would you like some breakfast? I fixed you something nice." He indicated the tray of food set across her abdomen. "We have a nice western omelet, sausage, toast and some orange juice. I didn't know whether you were a coffee drinker though, but just say the word and I'll brew you a fresh pot. It's all just a little service we provide here at chez Kyson's."

Michael pulled at her restraints again, not at all sure that she liked this vulnerable position.

"Ah. Ah. Ah. Not to worry. I have you nice and secure." He winked again. "I figured after breakfast, we could have a nice long talk about your situation."

"C'mon, Kyson. Cut it out. This isn't funny."

"Depends on what side of the handcuffs you're standing on," he said. He cut her a piece of the omelet and told her to open up.

Michael turned her head. "I'm not hungry. Unlock me."

"Aw, now. Don't be that way. I went to a lot of trouble cooking this breakfast. You don't want to be rude, do you?" He lifted the fork back to her lips and mimicked how he wanted her to open her mouth.

She eyed him wearily, but did as he instructed and took her first bite of breakfast.

"That's my girl." He actually patted her on the head and, perhaps for giggles, tweaked her left breast. "Now, if you eat all your breakfast, I might have a nice treat for you afterward."

Michael didn't know how to feel about this. It wasn't often that she didn't have control of a situation, the past week notwithstanding. "How long do you plan to keep me cuffed here?"

"For as long as it takes," he answered amicably. He lifted another bite of food to her mouth.

She chewed quickly but then started to choke.

"Easy now." He reached for a napkin and patted her awkwardly on the upper back. "None of that. It's time for me to get some answers."

"Is this how you do your interrogations?"

"I did get the idea from you," he admitted. "Pretty clever, don't you think?"

"I think you've lost your mind."

"In that case, it'll make us a perfect couple." He reached for the glass of orange juice and aided in tilting her head forward. "Easy."

Michael sipped. When he pulled the glass away, a few drops splattered against her right breast.

"Ah. Let me get that for you." Kyson leaned forward and lapped up the juice, taking his time licking her nipple until it glistened.

She closed her eyes, her breath thin in her chest while a throbbing ache pulsed between her legs.

"There. That's better," he said, lifting his head, then continuing to hand-feed her. "I have to say I had the most enjoyable time last night—or rather this morning. You truly do know how to make a man lose himself."

You're not so bad yourself, she refrained from saying aloud.

"I also have to tell you that you have to be one of the most intriguing women I've ever met," he said, studying her. "I'm drawn to you, but I don't trust you." He locked gazes with her. "What do you think I should do about that?"

How would she know? She had the same issue when it came to him.

"Ah. Maybe we're in the same position," he guessed correctly. "A stalemate."

The orange juice reappeared, and Michael carefully took another sip. This time, Kyson deliberately spilled it across her left breast.

"Oops." He set the glass down. "Looks like I made another mess."

Michael's stomach quivered in anticipation as he leaned forward and took her hardened bud into his greedy mouth. Hot flames licked at her insides while his tongue made lazy circles against the tip. As an added touch, his teeth nipped and chewed, sending delicious sensations racing through her body.

She sucked in a sharp breath. The ache between her legs spread to the center of her belly and then radiated outward toward her sensitive breasts. "Please," she begged on a ragged sigh.

Kyson lifted his head. Amusement twinkled in his eyes. "You know, I'm a bit hungry myself," he said, removing the tray from across her belly and exposing her naked body. "My. My. My," he whispered. "Now, this is a sight a man can get used to. What do you think?" His hands caressed her soft stomach and traveled down to graze the springy black curls between her legs.

She quivered.

"Do you think you can get used to waking every morning like this?"

"Cuffed to a bed?"

"Being worshipped by me?"

Her heart clenched.

"Do you think you could get used to me stroking you like this?" he asked, his fingers dipping in between her legs but not entering her. It felt as though he was tickling her with a feather. He'd captured her body's full attention.

"Maybe every morning I could rain kisses across every inch of you." He leaned down again, peppered kisses against her knee, her thigh and then against her lower lips. "Would you like to *belong* to me? Every woman wants to belong to someone, right?"

The very possibility caused her heart to race and unbidden tears to sting the back of her eyes. She hardly knew this man, and yet, she did know him.

Didn't she?

In just under a week, she knew he was a man who loved hard. He was a man who would change his life to avenge a loved one. He was a man who was hard not to trust. Right then she longed to tell him the truth, the whole truth regarding her ex-husband's disappearance. But then her own loyalty and protective nature toward her sisters stilled her lips.

If she went down, they would go down with her.

Kyson moved on, unfazed by her silence. In his

eyes, his gaze seemed to soak her in as if trying to memorize every curve of her body. He stood up, untied the belt of his robe. The moment the material parted, his sex sprang forward.

Immediately, Michael's hips rotated of their own accord.

"Anxious, are we?" he asked, but made no move toward her. He just reclaimed his spot on the edge of the bed. "Michael, tell me about your two friends, Ray and Scott Damon."

Michael drew a blank. She was so hot for him that she had trouble recalling her last name. "They're just old friends," she said.

"You have an interesting selection of friends," he said and kissed the inside of her thigh. "Do you normally befriend criminals?"

His tone sounded like he was inquiring about the weather or the time.

"We used to go to school together."

He nodded as if she'd given him the right answer. His head descended again; this time his mouth disappeared in the nest of curls between her legs.

"Ooh." She sighed at the first feel of his tongue delving inside her. After four long strokes, Michael's hips lifted four inches off the mattress.

"Did you have your friends kill your ex-husband?" he questioned in the same soft tone as before.

"No." She panted, too turned on to be offended. Kyson's eyes narrowed.

"I swear," she promised.

He seemed to accept the answer and dived again. Michael inched up the bed during her rewarded eight strokes.

"Have you told me the truth about everything?"

Michael didn't mean to hesitate. "I told you the truth about not having anything to do with my ex-husband's death," she stated. It was her way of avoiding a yes-or-no answer and she waited to see whether he would pick up on it.

Silence pulsed between them and it appeared he'd made a decision. He mouth reclaimed its position between her legs and, within a few more strokes of his powerful tongue, she was pitched over the edge of oblivion. She was lost to all thought and reason when he climbed in between her shackled legs and pushed inside of her.

The glorious hammering of his hips brought tears to her eyes. Rapture consumed her, heaven enfolded her and Kyson completed her.

Together, they caused the bed to jump and rattle against the bedroom wall. Kyson repeated her name against the shell of her ear. When his orgasm finally hit, he roared like a victorious animal in the wild and then collapsed.

Hot. Sweaty. And all hers.

Chapter 25

"We need to talk to someone in charge," Flex thundered.

A glorified receptionist with a badge stabbed Flex with an annoyed look. "Sir, we're doing the best we can. Please have a seat and someone will get back to you shortly."

"We have been waiting for someone for almost forty-five minutes," he stressed, leaning over the desk. "We need to speak to someone now. My sister is missing."

"Sir, you said so yourself that your sister has been missing for less than twenty-four hours. That doesn't make it high priority—especially when we are understaffed and overloaded. We work on a triage system and right now our officers are busy with priority cases."

Flex hammered a meaty fist against the desk. "This is serious! My sister's *life* may be in danger."

The short, stocky Korean officer didn't so much as flinch at Flex's outburst, but she laid out a warning. "Sir, if you don't calm yourself, I'm gonna have to ask you to leave. It's either that or I can find you a nice cell until you cool off."

"This is unbelievable," he raged.

"C'mon, Flex," Sheldon said, tugging on his arm. "Let's go back over here and wait."

They returned to a row of waiting chairs lined up against a bulletin board. The entire Adams clan, from babies to the grand patriarch, Marlin, filled the waiting area. The ones who weren't crying held the same worried expression.

After Michael didn't show up last night to the emergency family meeting, they all agreed first thing this morning to drive over to her place to see if their troubled sister was all right. They found the place ransacked. Whoever had broken into the place tore through it like a tornado. The Adamses feared Michael had gotten caught up in the crosshairs.

The stress of the situation nearly sent Peyton into early labor.

"Excuse me. Have you guys been helped?" a middle-aged African-American male officer inquired.

"Well, it's about time," Marlin grumbled.

"Yes, we're here to speak to someone about our missing sister," Flex said. "We've been waiting for nearly an hour."

The cop nodded his short, salt-and-pepper-colored head and directed them to come along with him. When the whole clan started to follow, he stopped. "I just need a couple of you guys," he said. "There won't be enough room for all of you."

The adults looked at one another and Sheldon made the decision that she, Frankie and Flex would follow the officer.

Marlin protested, but Sheldon assured him that everything would be all right. He nodded and returned to his seat to wait with the rest of the family.

"I'm Detective Dean Richards," the cop said, offering his hand to the threesome.

After they'd shaken hands, Richards directed them to take a seat. Since there was only one chair before his desk, the three siblings elected to remain standing.

Richards pecked on an ancient-looking computer. "You said you wanted to file a missing person's report?"

"Yes," the Adamses answered in unison and then looked at each other.

The officer bobbed his head and opened the appropriate screen. "Alrighty then. What is your sister's name?"

"Michael Adams," Sheldon said, and then rattled off her sister's address. However, before she could launch into her story, the cop held up his hand and frowned at the screen.

"What is it?" she inquired. "Is there a problem?"

"Uh. Just a minute," he said, pushing up from his chair. "Please wait right here."

When Richards scrambled away, the three Adams siblings glanced at each other again.

Frankie took the empty chair before Richards's desk and nibbled on her bottom lip. "This definitely can't be good."

Boldly, Flex leaned toward the cop's computer and read the screen. "I'd say. Her name is flashing. Must mean a red flag," he said.

"I should have popped a Xanax before coming here," Frankie muttered.

From across the station, they saw Richards approaching with two other officers trailing behind.

Frankie and Sheldon recognized Detective Griffin as he marched toward them.

"This is definitely *not* good," Sheldon stressed.

"Ladies." Griff smiled. "We meet again."

Each woman gave him a curt nod.

"If you don't mind following me," he said, "I'll take your statements."

"Why?" Flex asked. "This officer was helping us." He indicated Richards. "What's going on?"

"I'm sorry," Griff said. "I don't think we've met.

I'm Detective Robert Griffin and this here is my new partner, Detective Selena Martinez. And you are?"

"Flex Adams," he said, ignoring the officer's hand. "Michael is my sister."

"Ah, big family." Griff gave him the once-over and straightened his shoulders. "Well, Mr. Adams, I've had the pleasure of meeting three of your lovely sisters earlier this week when I was following up another missing person's report. Your ex-brother-in-law, I take it—Philip Matthews."

Flex understood now. His sisters had filled him in last night.

"So!" Griff clapped his hands. "If you all could follow me?" He turned without further ado and marched them to the back of the station.

Sheldon and Frankie reached for each other's hand in support. They knew without a doubt they were about to walk into the lion's den. "The only way to survive the impending ordeal was to tell the truth and that included the part in covering up Phil's kidnapping.

Juanita had never picked a lock in her life, but she was finding the experience exhilarating. With her entire Neighborhood Watch cronies stationed on the lookout, she worked the lock just as she'd read on the Internet.

The lock jumped and the door creaked open.

"We're in," Juanita said, excited.

Estelle clapped her hands while Beatrice stepped back and shook her head.

Juanita caught the action and rounded on her. "Oh, don't you go soft on me now. We're all in this together, remember?"

"All for one and one for all," Louise agreed, adjusting her wig. Heaven only knew why she didn't buy wigs that fit.

"Now, come on," Juanita said, waving them inside.

They entered the home of Philip Matthews on tiptoe. The house's eerie silence raised everyone's hackles.

"Now, whatever you do, don't *touch* anything," Estelle reminded them. "I learned that off *CSI*," she boasted proudly. "They can get fingerprints off the strangest things."

"Oh. I brought these," Louise said, reaching into her black purse and pulling out yellow latex gloves.

"Aren't those for washing dishes?" Estelle inquired, taking her pair.

"It was all I had around the house."

"Don't you girls care that we could go to jail for this?" Beatrice needled.

"Oh, stop it," Juanita said, slipping on her gloves. "We're not stealing anything. We're just taking a look around."

"But what are we looking for?"

"Anything out of the ordinary," she pressed.

Beatrice refrained from asking exactly what that would be. The place was still wrecked from when Phil's girlfriend reported him missing. How should they know what was and wasn't out of the ordinary?

Since she was the odd woman out in this detective adventure, she clammed up, not missing the irony that the neighborhood crime stoppers were actually committing the crime.

The four old ladies continued their slow creep throughout the house, their eyes straining for what they deemed out of the ordinary.

"You would have thought that his new girlfriend would've cleaned the place up a bit." Estelle sniffed.

"She probably didn't want to disturb evidence for the police."

"Police, hmmph." Juanita shook her head. "Phil turned up dead yesterday and the police haven't even come back to process the house yet."

"I see I'm not the only *CSI* fan," Estelle teased.

"Can we please get this over with?" Beatrice snapped.

Nothing turned up on the first floor, so Juanita led the group toward the staircase. Midway up, a strange stench burned their noses.

"What is that?" Juanita inquired. "It smells awful."

Beatrice froze on a stair. "I'm not going up there," she announced. "This is wrong nine ways to Sunday and you know it."

"Fine. You stand right there and we'll go check it out," Juanita said, not wanting to waste any more time arguing.

"Uh, I don't know," Louise spoke up. "Maybe I should stay here with her and keep her company."

"Are you kidding me?" Juanita asked. "We're already in here. We might as well go ahead and check it out."

Louise hesitated. "I don't know. Maybe we should stay in pairs. I think I saw that on *CSI*, too."

"You did not," Estelle refuted. "You made that up."

"Leave them here," Juanita said. "We're just wasting time."

Juanita and Estelle climbed the rest of the stairs, shaking their heads. They didn't have to travel too far to uncover the ungodly smell. The moment they opened the door to the master bedroom, they found what they were looking for: a dead body.

"You're not seriously going to leave me cuffed to the bed all day," Michael inquired, watching Kyson as he dressed.

"Not all day. I just want to go check out a few things."

After their morning of intense interrogation and exhausting sex, Kyson had tenderly given Michael a sponge bath, teasing and tickling as he did so. Afterward, he cruelly took a shower for himself.

"You can't be serious. You can't leave me like this."

"Don't worry. I'll cover you up so that you don't catch a chill."

"But what if I have to go to the bathroom or something?"

"I won't be gone long," he promised. "An hour, two tops."

"This isn't funny!"

Despite her temper, Kyson smiled, leaned over the bed and kissed her. "Like I said, it depends on what side of the cuffs you're on."

"At least uncuff my feet."

He glanced down, gave it serious consideration and then agreed. "All right." He walked to the dresser across the room and retrieved a small key.

When he released her legs, Michael immediate curled up to get more comfortable. "What am I going to do if something happens to you and I'm locked like this?"

"Better hope that nothing happens to me." He chuckled.

Her eyes narrowed.

"Look, I'm just going to go check out a few things. See if anyone else has seen this SUV you told me about, run the description of the kidnappers by Griff and my brother at his agency."

"Basically, you're just going to go check out whether I told you the truth."

"All of it?"

"Yes," she lied.

He shrugged with a lighthearted smile. "It is a strange story. It would've helped if you'd gotten a tag number or something. Who knows, maybe I'll swing by Sunnyvale and talk to those Damon twins."

Michael sat up. "What? Why?"

"Ah. That got your attention." His smile disappeared. "If you've told the truth, what will it hurt?"

"Kyson, uncuff me."

"I will," he said. "When I return." He headed toward the door. "Who knows? If your story checks out—" his eyes dragged over her covered body "—maybe we can see what we can do about lunch."

Chapter 26

"Let me get this straight," Detective Martinez said, staring incredulously at the Adams clan across the table. "You're telling me that your sister, Michael Adams, had her ex-husband kidnapped?"

"Inadvertently," Sheldon corrected, glancing over at Frankie.

"Yeah. It was more like she casually mentioned that she'd like to have her ex-husband killed," Frankie said.

"She hired hit men?" Martinez questioned, stunned.

"No. No. Not at all," the girls tried to backtrack.

"Uh-huh." Martinez's gaze bounced between the

two women. "So!" She drew a deep breath and tried to recap. "Michael Adams *inadvertently* let it slip that she wanted to…*harm* her ex. Is that better?"

Sheldon straightened. "See. You have to understand that she was drunk at the time," she offered the excuse again. "It was a bitter divorce and I guess you could say that she was still a little hurt."

"So she wanted to kill him." Martinez kept leading the conversation back to murder.

"Yes, but she didn't really *mean* it." Frankie laughed. "If anything, she was joking."

"Joking?" Griff cut in. "This joke sure does have a deadly punch line."

"That's just how Michael is," Sheldon explained. "I'm sure if you were to ask around the department, there are plenty of officers who've had dealings with my sister in the past. She's a prankster."

"Oh, we've read her record," Martinez said. "It's definitely interesting reading."

"Right," Flex said. "It's never been anything serious. Hell, it's been years since she's been in here. She's calmed down considerably."

"Actually—" Griff turned to a thick folder "—it says here she was arrested a year ago in Los Angeles for breaking and entering a prominent doctor's residence and vandalizing the place."

Flex frowned. "She was?"

"Her and a Joseph Adams—another sister, I take it?"

"Well, yeah," Sheldon said. "But that shouldn't count. Joey was dating the doctor when he just up and dumped her on Valentine's Day and then said he was marrying someone else."

"So you ladies tend to become criminals when men break up with you, is that it?" Martinez concluded.

"Not hardened criminals," Frankie said. "Just… you know, those things are just tactics women use all the time to get a little revenge. Surely you've been there before." She tried smoothing her over with a smile. "You're not going to tell me you've never keyed an ex-boyfriend's car or added a little sugar in the tank or even bleached his clothes when one of them has done you wrong."

Martinez cleared her throat. "We're not discussing me."

Griffin cast a sideways glance.

"I can say, however, that it *is* unusual to set a couple of thugs out to kidnap an ex."

"Okay, I'll give you that," Sheldon said. "But to Ray and Scott's defense they were also drinking that night. They weren't thinking clearly. They were just helping out an old friend."

Flex finally jumped back into the conversation. "Girls, I don't think you're helping this situation."

"Oh. I'd say they are shedding quite a lot of light on this case," Griff said, stretching his limbs beneath the table. "Basically what you're saying is that when we talked to you about Phil Matthews six days ago, he was actually, at that moment, tied and gagged in your sister's basement?"

"Right." Sheldon winced.

"And you didn't tell us that because…?"

"You would have hauled us to jail," Sheldon said, stating the obvious.

"I'd like to go on record and say that I didn't know he was down there until after you guys left."

"Frankie!" Sheldon elbowed her.

"What? It's the truth."

"Anyway—" Sheldon turned her attention back to the officers "—Michael didn't even know he was down there until she went down to the basement for coffee."

Griff remembered the incident well. Michael had returned upstairs behaving strangely—not that she wasn't odd beforehand. "The whole rat infestation," he said.

"Right!" Frankie perked up. "You remember."

"It's sort of hard to forget." He leaned back into his chair. "I have a feeling you ladies are going to be quite memorable for years to come."

"Anyway," Sheldon said, "after you left, we went downstairs to untie him and explain to Phil that it had all been a huge mistake and misunderstanding."

"So you just released him and he went on his merry little way?" Martinez said.

"Not exactly." Frankie glanced at her sister. "See, Phil wasn't exactly in the best of moods—"

"Can't blame him there," Flex mumbled and then quieted when his sisters shot him a quelling look.

"Anyway," Frankie continued, "him being hot under the collar, he began shouting and threatening to have us arrested."

Griff and Martinez leaned over the table. "Go on," they said.

"Well, we tried to make him see reason, but he just remained belligerent until Michael came up with the idea that perhaps he'd calm down once he'd heard from the two horses' mouths that it had all been a misunderstanding." She shrugged. "So… we put him in the trunk of Michael's car and drove him to our sister Peyton's house."

"The trunk?"

The girls nodded.

They had successfully silenced the two officers.

"I know this all *sounds* bad."

"A little," Griff said.

"Damn." Martinez groaned. "How many sisters are there?"

"Six," Flex said flatly. "One is just a year old."

"You poor man," Griff said, shaking his head.

"Look, we were only trying to explain what happened," Sheldon said.

"By shoving a tied-and-gagged man into the trunk of a car?"

"Well, when you say it like that." Frankie rolled her eyes.

"How do you prefer I say it?"

"It doesn't matter," Flex said, rubbing his forehead. "The point is that Phil was alive when the girls last saw him."

"According to them."

"And my brother-in-law, Lincoln Carver," Flex said.

"He's involved in this, too?" Martinez asked, struggling to keep up.

"Inadvertently," Sheldon clarified.

"Well, of course."

"Lincoln didn't know what was going on," Frankie said, "but he was the one to tell us that he saw Phil escaping the car."

"So you see, when we didn't hear from Phil, we thought he'd simply calmed down and was willing to let the whole incident go."

"That would have been very big of him," Griff commented.

"It wasn't until yesterday when his death was splashed all over the news that we knew what really happened."

Griff rubbed his palms over his face and drew a deep breath. "Let's say that we believe this story, why didn't your sister tell us this yesterday?"

"Yeah," Martinez cut in. "Why stick to the lie that she hadn't seen Matthews for weeks?"

The family tossed a look around.

"I'd imagine she was trying to protect us," Sheldon said.

"Plus," Frankie added, "we probably frightened her into believing no one would believe our story."

"Oh, I don't know," Martinez said. "I still believe in Santa Claus and the Tooth Fairy."

"Look, lady," Frankie said, getting up. "The point of the matter is, Phil was alive when we last saw him. And now that Michael is missing and her house has been ransacked, we can't help but feel her life may be in danger."

"Normally," Griff said, "this would be the time we would ask whether your sister had any known enemies, but I'm almost afraid you'll hand over the entire White Pages."

"Funny," Sheldon said drily.

"Thanks."

"My sister may have some enemies, but no one that would want her harmed—much. She really is a very lovable person—once you get to know her."

There was a knock on the door before Captain Harris poked his head inside and zeroed in on his two officers. "Can I see you two in my office for a moment?"

"Right away," Griff and Martinez chorused.

Pushing his chair back and climbing to his feet, Griff said, "You guys make yourselves comfortable. We'll be right back."

Griff and Martinez quickly marched out of the interrogation room.

"Can you believe that family?" Martinez chuckled.

"People like them keep the job interesting."

"Yo, Griff," Richards shouted from across the room. "Need to talk to you."

"Can it keep? On my way to the captain's office."

"It's about the Matthews case."

He stopped. "What about it?"

"Dispatch just took a call from a hysterical neighbor. Said they found a second body at the vic's house."

"Don't tell me this chick just upgraded to a serial killer," Martinez said, awed.

Griff shook his head. "At this point nothing surprises me." He then shouted back to Richards. "Thanks for the 411." He continued toward the captain's office, when his cell phone buzzed against his hip. "Busy morning," he mumbled. Retrieving the phone, he glanced at the ID screen and almost let it go to voice mail, when he had a change of heart. "Hey, buddy. Now is not a good time. It's crazy around here."

"Tell me about it," Kyson said. "I need a favor."

"It's gonna have to wait. I'm working on the Matthews case."

"You got a break?"

"Something like that." He chuckled. "Michael Adams's sisters are in here confessing to kidnapping the man. Can you believe it? The whole time we were talking to them about Matthews's disappearance, the man was tied and gagged in the basement. Classic."

"What?"

"Yeah." Griff stopped. "Hey, buddy. You're not still messing around with her, are you? Hello? Kyson, are you there? Hello?"

Kyson disconnected the call and swore under his breath. She had done it again. She had played him a fool. He pulled the car over to the side of the road and roared up at its roof. He had the overwhelming urge to punch something.

Anything.

He allowed himself a private tirade when he'd laid into the car's horn. He couldn't believe it. He'd actually started to believe her.

Damn it.

After about ten minutes, he rolled down the car window and breathed in the thick California air. Finally, he calmed a bit.

A mile from the Damon twins' address, Kyson considered going back and confronting Michael. He debated awhile and then pulled his car back into traffic.

Ray and Scott Damon were packing to get the hell out of Dodge. It worried them that Michael never showed yesterday, but it wasn't until the breaking news of a body being discovered at Phil Matthews's residence that the brothers decided that it was worth violating the terms of their probation to get out of California.

"Do you think that she would drop dime on us?" Scott asked while he continued packing his bags.

"Man, I don't even know this chick anymore. What kind of stuff does she have us involved in?"

"You were the one with the idea of helping her out."

"Yeah, but I'm thinking she knew we would help," Ray said, convinced. "That was why she sidled up next to us that night. The nerve."

"I can't believe she'd set us up. After all we've been through in the past." He threw a couple of shirts into a bag, grabbed his favorite sneakers and looked around the place. "Think that's enough. We don't have time to pack everything."

The brothers couldn't believe the situation they'd found themselves in as they raced out the apartment and toward their black SUV.

Kyson pulled into the small apartment complex, immediately catching sight of the large twins jumping into a black Ford Explorer. "Well, I'll be damned."

He whipped his car into a parking space and reached beneath the car seat for his private registered gun. It was time to get some answers.

* * *

Naomi entered her brother's home, anxious to see his surprised face when he saw her. Since his car wasn't parked outside, she hoped it meant she had time to take a shower and grab a nap before he returned. She hated that she couldn't arrive in time for his birthday, but she thought it was better late than never.

Walking through the living room toward the staircase, she stopped when she caught sight of a woman's bra sprawled across the carpet.

"Celibate my ass." She chuckled. "Boys will be boys." As she climbed the staircase and past the master bedroom, a woman's voice floated out to her.

"Kyson?"

Naomi stopped. Who on earth?

"Uh, no. It's Naomi," she answered awkwardly. "I'm, uh, Kyson's sister. I came in for a surprise visit. Uh, I'm sorry to disturb you. I'm just going to put my things in the guest room."

"Oh, please. Could you help me?"

Naomi frowned and inched toward the door. "Is something wrong?"

"Well, sort of," the woman said.

Curious, Naomi set her bags down and then pushed open the door. Whatever she was expecting, finding a barely covered woman handcuffed to the bed wasn't it. "What on earth is going on in here?"

Chapter 27

Detectives Griffin and Martinez stormed through the interrogation room and barked orders to the Adams clan.

"Up against the wall and place your hands behind your head."

"What?" Sheldon jumped from her seat and stared at the officers in disbelief. "You're arresting us?"

Martinez spun Frankie around to face the wall and gave the command again. "Hands behind your head."

"Mr. Adams, you're free to go," Griff said. "At this moment we don't have anything to charge you with—at the moment. But don't go far."

"Can you please explain what's going on?" Flex thundered. "Why are you arresting my sisters?"

"Ouch," Sheldon complained when Martinez slapped the cuffs on her.

"Hey, take it easy," Flex demanded and then turned back toward Griff. "I don't understand. We came to you guys."

"Yeah, confessing to kidnapping a murdered man," Griff said.

"Mr. Adams, I'm going have to ask you again to leave."

"Not until you tell me what's going on. You guys are supposed to go out and look for my sister, Michael."

"Oh, we're looking for her all right."

"You have the right to remain silent. Anything you say can and will be held against you in a court of law," Martinez recited to the women. "You have the right to an attorney…"

"This isn't right," Flex insisted.

"Sir, your sisters are being charged with kidnapping and accessories to murder."

"We told you," Frankie said, nearing hysterics. "We didn't kill anybody. Hell, we didn't *really* kidnap Phil."

"That's for a jury to decide," Griff said. "Sir, please leave."

"Sheldon, Frankie, don't worry I'm going to get you out of here," he assured, heading toward the door.

"Call Billingsley," Frankie pleaded. "Tell him to get his butt down here."

Flex nodded. "I'm on it." He rushed out the interrogation room, but was delivered another shocker when he reached the waiting area.

Right there in the front of the station, his extremely pregnant sister, Peyton, and her husband, Lincoln, were being arrested.

Marlin looked near ready to have a stroke. "Someone tell me what the hell is going on! I want answers!" He saw his son approaching and he raced forward. "What's happening? Where are Sheldon and Frankie?"

"Pop, I'll tell you later. Let's get the kids out of here."

"No! You tell me what's going on!"

An officer cleared his throat. The two men whirled around.

Griff stood with a terse look. "Mr. Adams," he said to Flex. "If you know where your sister Michael is, I suggest you tell her to turn herself in."

"What in the hell do you mean 'if we know'?" Marlin stepped before his son. "That's the damn reason we came here. She's missing, you idiot!"

Unfazed, Griff continued, "We located Michael's car parked at the Great Mall. Our crime techs have processed it and found blood that matches our vic, Phil Matthews."

Marlin paled and then clutched at his arm.

"Sir." Griff blinked. "Sir, are you all right?"

Flex turned toward his father and noted how he struggled for breath. "Someone, call an ambulance," Flex shouted. "I think he's having a heart attack!"

"Step out of the vehicle," Kyson shouted, his gun leveled on the Damon that was behind the wheel.

"Aw, man. This is some bullshit."

"Open the door and then put your hands in the air," Kyson commanded. The driver moved slowly, but did as he was told though hostility glimmered in his eyes.

"Forget this," the Damon in the passenger seat said, bolting out of his door to take up running down the parking lot.

When Kyson swung his gun toward the running man, the Damon in front of him capitalized on the mistake by delivering a hard chop against the back of Kyson's neck. Stars exploded before him and he dropped his gun. Before he could recover, the muscular Damon sent a hard punch across his jaw.

Since Kyson had been taken by surprise, he sustained a few hard blows before he finally sent his own sucker punch into Damon twin number one's hard abs.

"Oomph!" The man folded at his waist.

Kyson straightened and then delivered a powerful blow across the man's jaw.

Damon fell to one knee and struggled to get back up.

Now jabbing a one-two punch, Kyson watched the man fall flat on his back.

Out of nowhere, sirens pierced the air and a line of Sunnyvale police cars screeched into the complex parking lot, surrounding Kyson, the fallen Damon and even Damon number two down the parking lot.

Immediately, Kyson threw his hands up in the air.

Michael pushed past her embarrassment at being caught in a highly compromising position, but she was more than grateful to Kyson's younger sister for popping up when she did.

Now dressed, she rushed to the phone and struggled to remember the number she'd scrawled across her palm yesterday. She needed to warn the Damon twins of Kyson's visit. She hated to think how the men might react to a cop showing up unexpectedly. Why, oh, why didn't she go see them yesterday so they could get their stories straight?

When the phone just rang, Michael's gut twisted into knots. Was she too late?

She hardly heard a word from the jabbering Naomi Dekker. "So how long have you and my brother been dating?"

"What?" Michael finally caught one of the girl's questions and frowned. "We're not exactly dating," she said.

"Oh." Naomi's eyes raked over her and then glowed with a new understanding.

"It's not like that, either," Michael said, not wanting her to think that she was a hooker or something. "Let's just say that my and your brother's relationship is complicated."

A smile returned to Naomi's face. "All of his relationships are." She perked up when Michael grabbed her bag. "Are you leaving?"

"Uh, yeah." Michael glanced around, spotted her bra from last night and grabbed it. "I don't want to intrude on a brother-and-sister reunion. Just, um, tell him I'll call him later," she lied. Chances were if Kyson ever saw her again, he'd probably try to throttle her for lying to him. She was on her own to solve Phil's murder.

"Well, all right," Naomi said, smiling. "Goodbye."

"Bye." Michael slammed the door behind her and raced down the sidewalk in a rush to get out of the apartment complex.

In a flash, sirens filled the air and a team of police cars surrounded her. She stopped cold, dropped her bag and threw her hands into the air.

She recognized the cops jumping out of the first vehicle in front of her: Detectives Griffin and Martinez.

"Michael Adams," Martinez said, approaching. "Please get down and place your hands behind your back."

Heart racing, Michael followed the cop's instructions. When she lay flat against the concrete, Martinez approached and slapped a different pair of handcuffs on her wrist—one that bit into her skin.

"You have the right to remain silent. Anything you say can and will be held against you in a court of law…"

Tears splashed down Michael's face as she listened to the rights being read to her. When she was done, several pairs of hands aided in getting her to her feet. From the corner of her eyes, she saw Kyson standing behind a cop car and watching her arrest.

The look on his face ripped out her heart as she was led to a patrol car, but before Michael was shoved inside, she mouthed the words *I'm so sorry*.

Kyson's face turned to stone a second before he turned and walked away.

Chapter 28

The Trial...

"Please place your hand on the Bible and raise your right hand," the bailiff instructed.

Michael's hand sprang into the air.

"Please state your whole name," the stoic bailiff droned.

"Michael Anthony Adams," she said nervously and then cleared the boulder blocking her windpipe. If anything, she made it worse.

"Do you solemnly swear to tell the truth, the whole truth and nothing but the truth so help you God?"

"I—I do." Damn. Why had she stuttered? Her gaze shattered across the crowded courtroom to access the damage—nothing but a wall of stony faces and accusatory gazes stared back at her.

They are going to give me the death sentence!

"You may be seated," Judge Carter said, turning in her seat so that Michael had her full attention.

Michael lowered herself into the witness seat while the bailiff returned to his post and District Attorney Harold Joplin approached the witness stand in an impressive suit.

"Good morning, Ms. Adams," he greeted with a smile that missed his eyes.

Not sure she could trust her voice just yet, Michael just gave him a curt nod and forced herself to sit up straight. She didn't dare look to the front-row bench behind the defense. No doubt the sight of her family, minus her father, fidgeting in their seats with openly terrified expressions would bring on the tears again. Her father's death left a gaping whole in their lives. The guilt of her father's fatal heart attack was something that would haunt Michael for the rest of her life. Frankly, they had done enough crying throughout this exhausting trial.

"Ms. Adams, did you kill your ex-husband?" Joplin asked, wasting no time getting to the nitty-gritty.

"Absolutely not!" she stated emphatically.

A loud wave of gasps and murmurs rose from the courtroom spectators.

What had everyone expected? That she'd agreed to take the stand so that she could throw herself on the mercy of the court?

A smile finally lit Joplin's blue eyes as if he was going to relish his time nailing her to the wall.

Michael didn't want to, but she couldn't stop herself from shooting a daggerlike gaze over to Detective Kyson Dekker.

Kyson's polished black orbs met her gaze unblinkingly. The heat radiating from them caused her to look away first.

"Ms. Adams," Joplin thundered, slicing through the tension between the police officer and the defendant. "Do you know Ray and Scott Damon—otherwise known as the Damon twins?"

She cleared her throat again, but the boulder still refused to budge. "I—I do." Damn. She did it again.

"Do you recall Ray and Scott Damon testifying before this jury that it was *you* who had told them that you wanted to kill your ex-husband?"

Her back grew even straighter remembering those two idiots on the stand mixing fact with fiction. "I do recall that."

Joplin braided his well-manicured fingers together while he began a slow pace before the witness stand. "Do you also recall Ray and Scott Damon telling this court that it was *you* who'd told them exactly how to break into your ex-husband's house, how to bypass the security system and even how they could cover their tracks?"

Michael drew in a deep breath. Did she really have to answer the smug attorney's questions?

"Answer the question, Ms. Adams," Judge Carter directed after Michael's long insolent silence.

"Of course I do."

"Then is it your testimony that Ray and Scott Damon perjured themselves here at this court?"

She drew another deep breath, cast a look to her four fidgeting sisters.

"Ms. Adams," the judge cut in again.

"No," Michael answered softly.

"I'm sorry, Ms. Adams," Joplin said. "Could you please speak up? I'm not sure everyone in the jury heard your answer."

"I said no. Ray and Scotty didn't lie."

The court erupted with a loud din of whispering.

Michael had a sudden premonition of being strapped to a cold steel table and waiting to be administered a lethal injection.

"Order in the court!" Judge Carter rapped her gavel. "Order!"

Slowly, the voices lowered to disjointed whispers.

Joplin was finally in his element, preening like a peacock.

"I told them how to kidnap Philip, not kill him."

"They didn't kill him. *You* did."

Michael jumped to her feet. "That's a lie!"

"I object!" Billingsley finally woke up from his nap in time to participate in the proceedings.

The court was abuzz again.

"Order! Order!" The judge rapped her gavel again and then told Michael, "Please remain seated, Ms. Adams."

Michael did as she was told, but continued to glare at the district attorney while simultaneously coaching herself to remain calm.

"No more questions," Joplin said, smirking his way back to his seat.

Billingsley stumbled to his feet and pushed up a pair of glasses that were as thick as old Coca-Cola bottles. "Ms. Adams," he said in a thick Louisiana accent and rubbing a hand across his wiry cotton hair. "The court has heard the Damon twins' version of events. Maybe you should give everyone here your side of the story."

Michael bobbed her head and flashed a pleading look in Detective Dekker's direction. True, it was imperative that she convince the jury of her innocence, but no one's opinion meant more than Kyson's.

Mainly because during the course of the past crazy months, he'd come to mean more to her than life itself.

Michael met Kyson's onyx gaze, once again charging the room with undeniable electricity. Perhaps it was the hard, stubborn set of his jaw that caused tears to burn her eyes.

"Ms. Adams?" Billingsley prompted.

"Yes," Michael said, pulled herself together and started her story from the beginning. Halfway through her version of events, she stole a glance at the jury and knew she was in trouble.

"Do you solemnly swear to tell the truth, the whole truth and nothing but the truth so help you God?"

"I do," Kyson affirmed, his deep baritone rumbling through the courtroom. He then removed his hand from the Bible and took his seat.

He'd promised himself that once he was on the witness stand he would keep his attention focused on the examining attorneys and far away from where Michael sat, watching him. However, that vow proved to be harder to keep than he'd expected.

Her dark chestnut-colored eyes were like two hypnotic magnets that drew his gaze to the defense table the moment he took his seat. The subsequent pain in his heart was a direct result of witnessing the absolute misery and hurt reflected in her eyes.

In the time they'd known each other so much had transpired between them: distrust, lies and even love.

Love.

When the word drifted across his mind, it made him pause. He'd chosen a hell of time and place to realize that he loved her. But who chose such things?

"Detective Dekker, you were here in court yesterday when Ms. Michael Adams came to the stand, were you not?" the district attorney asked as he approached.

"I was."

"Does Ms. Adams's rendition of your first meeting match your own of that day?"

"It does," Kyson answered, but didn't like how Joplin's smile appeared calculated and manufactured.

"Detective, was that your one and only encounter with Ms. Adams?"

A flash of Michael's naked body rubbing against his flashed inside of his head. A brief audio clip of her melodic moans and his heavy sighs filled his ears.

"Detective Dekker?"

Kyson blinked and then coughed to cover his embarrassment. "No, it was not."

Joplin nodded. "Then maybe you could tell this court your version of the events leading up to the arrest of the defendant."

Kyson's gaze drifted back over to Michael, but this time she kept her gaze averted. That only deepened his pain and heartache because his testimony would likely get her the death penalty.

Chapter 29

Juanita and her Neighborhood Watch gang were local celebrities. Discovering Michael Adams's second victim, Vanessa Delaney, in Phil Matthews's home, news agencies seemed to get a kick out of the older ladies' crime-fighting abilities. Now that Michael's trial was under way, they were once again thrown into the limelight for their opinion on the proceedings.

"I knew the girl was trouble the first time I laid eyes on her," Juanita said, sitting on her sofa in her living room. "Mrs. Matthews—that was her name back then—always had trouble conforming to the rules and regulations of our fine Home Owner's

Association. I just think that it's a pity that her ex-husband didn't see the kind of woman she truly was—and that poor, poor woman she killed out of blind jealousy when she realized Phil had moved on. I read somewhere that he and Ms. Delaney used to work together at his old job—Initech—or something like that. My friend Estelle said they build top-secret stuff for the government, weapons or something like that for the military. Anyway, Phil had a brilliant mind. Such a loss," she said sadly into the cameras.

"Why, it seems like yesterday he was just fooling around in the backyard. He was a master gardener, you know. We shared many secrets. He would even run errands for me, even though he was a *very* busy man. He'd work long hours. Of course, now I know he was likely working those long hours so he could stay away from that crazy wife of his."

"So you definitely believe that Ms. Adams had a hand in his murder?" the reporter asked.

"They wouldn't have arrested her if she wasn't guilty," Juanita said flatly. "I just regret our little Neighborhood Watch couldn't have done more to prevent those senseless crimes." She shook her head. "You know, I was the one who saw those evil twins taking off in their getaway car that night." She sighed. "The last time I saw Phil…"

"The last time what?" the reporter nudged.

"Well, the last time I saw him, he gave me a

package he wanted me to hold for him. Said it was a gift or something like that. Hmmph. I'd forgotten about that. I just stored it in the basement and plum forgot about it. I probably need to contact his next of kin or something."

The man punched the off button on the television and turned toward his partner. "Did you just hear that?"

"I heard and I can't believe it."

"Do you think…?"

"It has to be. We've searched everywhere else."

"You think our old employer will still be interested in our retrieving it?"

"It'll definitely make up how we botched the job," the woman said.

A smile slithered across the killer's lips. "I'll be damned. It looks like we're back in business."

After a long day in court, Kyson arrived home emotionally and mentally exhausted. Now that he'd quit the force, he'd taken a job with his brother at K.D. Dekker Investigative Services.

The job wasn't as bad as Khail had led him to believe. The pay fluctuated, but it was enough to help him complete the last few classes to get his engineering degree.

It broke Khail's heart when Kyson announced he was retiring from fighting, too. After all, it was

Khail's dream, not his. He still frequented King's Gym, mainly to relieve much of the stress of the trial. Watching the proceedings was much harder than he dreamed it would be. Seeing Michael on the stand and sticking to her story about not killing her ex-husband and his girlfriend.

She and the Damon twins admitted to the kidnapping fiasco, and the Adams sisters had all stuck to their guns about Phil escaping the trunk of Michael's car alive. Then again, the guilty often stuck to a lie until they were about to receive the needle.

Kyson's heart lurched. Michael could receive the death penalty.

Thinking of the possibilities was more than he could stand most days. He walked into the kitchen, grabbed two beers and proceeded to drink them one after the other. It was hard being in the apartment sometimes. Remembering the night that he brought her to his place haunted him.

He'd only been in love twice in his life. One woman was murdered and the second one could be put to death.

Life had a funny way of sucker punching him.

Kyson stopped and thought about the word *love* drifting around in his head. Had he really fallen in love with Michael Adams? Who fell in love that fast?

Cared—yes.

Love?

He shook the word out of his head and commanded himself not to think about it anymore. Yet, he knew it was an order he couldn't carry out.

There was a rap on the door before Khail breezed inside.

"Man, when are you going to stop busting in here like you're paying rent?"

Khail laughed and made his way to the refrigerator to retrieve his own beer. "Hell, I keep thinking one day *I'm* going to discover a naked woman cuffed to your bed."

Kyson rolled his eyes. Naomi never missed an opportunity to remind him of that day either.

"Besides," Khail said, "after today, I thought you needed the company." He popped open his beer. "How did it go on the witness stand?"

"I don't want to talk about it."

"That bad, huh?"

Instead of answering, Kyson nodded.

"Tough break, bro." Khail took a long pull on his beer. When he came up for air, he pounded a hand against Kyson's back. "I hope this experience hasn't scared you off from jumping back into the dating pool. So you fell for a murderer, it's not the end of the world."

"They haven't proved that she killed anybody."

"Ah. Still holding out hope, huh?"

Kyson didn't answer.

There was another rap at the door.

"Hey, a party," Khail said.

Kyson moaned. "Khail, please say that you didn't invite women over here."

"Now, what kind of brother would I be if I let you sulk over a locked-down jailbird?"

"I'm not interested in any of your silicone bimbos."

"Hey, bimbos need love, too."

Khail walked to the front door and pulled it open, only to discover it wasn't the girls he'd invited. "Ah, Detective Griffin. Long time no see."

Griff chuckled and entered the apartment. "How's it hanging, Khail?"

"Hanging low, bro. It's hanging low."

Griff walked into the living room and saw Kyson standing by the kitchen counter.

"Hey, buddy!"

"What's up?" Kyson said, joining him in the living room. "What brings you by here? Don't tell me you thought I needed cheering up, too."

Griff shared a half smile. "Saw you on the stand today, looking like a thrown-away puppy."

"Naw. Naw." Khail moaned. "Did he go out like that?" He shook his head. "Damn shame. Can I get you a beer?"

"Khail," Kyson said, "you're making yourself a little too comfortable."

"What? You should offer the man a drink. I can't help it if you have bad manners." Khail disappeared into the kitchen.

Griff flashed a smile. "So, how *are* you doing?"

Kyson shrugged. "Hanging in there."

"That's good. That's good."

"How are you and Martinez working out?" Kyson continued with the niceties.

"Good. Good. Of course, she has the hots for me."

"Dreaming again?"

"It's a nice dream."

The old partners laughed as Khail rejoined them and handed Griff his beer.

"Care to sit down?" Kyson asked, though he was hardly in the mood for company.

"Don't mind if I do." Griff took a seat on the sofa.

"Look, Kyson," Griff said suddenly. "I didn't just come to see if you were all right."

"Oh?"

"Yeah. I also wanted to talk to you about something."

"Shoot." Kyson drained the last of his beer.

"It's about the Damon twins and their Ford Explorer."

"What about it?"

"Well, when the Damon twins were arrested, I bought into the story that they and Michael were in on this thing together."

Kyson shifted in his chair. "Yeah. That's what we all concluded."

"Michael's testimony about a black SUV chasing her around reminded me of something."

"Aw. The alleged kidnappers slash killers she talks about."

"When it came to light the Damon twins owned a black SUV, I figured it was them I saw tailing her the day before her arrest, but the thing is, I'd gotten a tag number, but never got a chance to run it through DMV."

"So?"

"Well, I came across the tag number again in my notepad and…it doesn't match the Damon twins' Ford Explorer."

Kyson let his friend's words sink in. "What are you saying?"

"That it wasn't the Damon twins I saw chasing her. It was someone else."

At promptly nine o'clock, Juanita climbed into bed. She'd had a full and productive day and tomorrow she would be called on the stand in the Michael Adams trial. She planned to show no mercy and tell the court that she thought her ex-neighbor absolutely capable of murder.

As she did every night, she reached over to the nightstand, picked up her reading glasses and grabbed her latest and greatest crime novel. Before she could dive into the pages, the walkie-talkie chirped beside her.

"Spring Bird to Momma Bird, come in. Over."

Juanita picked up the walkie-talkie and responded, *"Momma Bird here, come in. Whatcha got, George? Over."*

"Just checking in to let you know that I'm officially on duty. Over."

"Very good. You make sure you stay awake tonight. Louise said she caught you sleeping on the job last week. Over."

"I told her that was an adverse reaction to some new medication my doctor prescribed. I can do my job. Over."

Juanita rolled her eyes. *"No need to get all huffy, George. I was just saying. Let somebody know if you need for them to take over. Over."*

"No need. I'm definitely on the job. Over."

"All right. Have a good night. Over." She placed the walkie-talkie on the nightstand and returned her attention to her book. Thirty minutes later, her eyes grew heavy and she put the book and her glasses away.

It felt as if she'd just drifted off when she heard the chirp of the walkie-talkie.

"Spring Bird to Momma Bird, are you up, Juanita? Over."

Groggily, Juanita opened her eyes.

"Spring Bird to Momma Bird, please come in. Over."

Juanita sat up, annoyed, and reached for the chirping walkie-talkie. This had better be good. *"Momma Bird here. What is it, George?"*

"*You forgot to say over. Over.*"

"*Oh, will you just tell me what's wrong? Over.*"

"*Uh, yeah. I was wondering if you were in your bedroom.*"

"*What? Please tell me that's not really why you're paging me. Why on earth do you need to know where I am? Over!*"

"*Well, if I'm not mistaken, your basement light just came on.*"

Chapter 30

Instead of locking herself in her bedroom and waiting for the police like the 911 operator on the phone on the nightstand table told her to do, Juanita grabbed her glasses, climbed out of her bed and went to her closet. She drew her deceased husband's old .44 Magnum firearm. Her husband had bought it because he was such a big fan of the movie *Dirty Harry*.

For the most part, the gun hadn't been out of the box more than a few times. However, Juanita experienced an incredible surge of power holding the weapon. She took her time checking to make sure it was loaded and then took a longer amount of time trying to remember how to turn the safety off.

If she had to aim this sucker at somebody, she wanted to make sure she could fire it. Certain she was ready to take on any danger, Juanita pulled open her bedroom door, peeked out and crept out into the dark house.

Her small footsteps were silent in the thick, plush carpet. It seemed to take forever to make her way from her bedroom, down the stairs, across the foyer, through the living room and over to the basement door.

She couldn't tell whether the fierce racing of her heart was from fear or excitement. This was what it was like to be a real detective. Her hand landed on the door, when a sound from the kitchen caught her attention.

Were they in the basement or were they in the kitchen? She was confused. Leave it to George to get the facts wrong. At no time did it occur to Juanita to return to her bedroom.

Heavy footsteps moved around in the kitchen and then headed toward the door.

Juanita wondered what she should do. She only had a second to think about finding a hiding place before a very large and muscular black man appeared in the dining/kitchen archway.

"What the—"

At the same time, the basement door opened and

an Asian woman rushed through, whispering, "I found it. Damn son of a bitch Matthews had it stashed here this whole—"

The woman turned when she saw her partner wasn't looking at her.

Juanita lifted the heavy gun, now thinking that it weighed a ton. "Don't move! The police are on their way."

"Now, now," the man said, approaching.

Juanita backed up, but held the gun firmly in her hands. Why in the hell had she thought this a good idea?

"Why don't you put that thing down before you hurt somebody," the man said.

It was clear he was not afraid of her and Juanita read something in his eyes that warned her if he ever got hold of the gun, she was a dead woman.

"Nobody is going to hurt you. Put the gun down and me and my friend will just leave."

For the first time Juanita noticed the box in the woman's hand. Phil's box. The one he'd asked for her to keep in her basement. Why would they want that?

Could it be that she had this whole thing wrong?

"You killed Phil," she accused. "Didn't you?

"That Michael has been telling the truth about you two. You tried to kidnap her and kill her—just like she's been saying in court. You killed that Delaney girl, too. Didn't you?"

Neither of her intruders said a word.

In a space of a minute, Juanita had put it all together. "What is it?" she asked. "What's in that box?"

"It belongs to us," the woman sniped. "Our bosses paid for it and we're going to make sure that they get it."

The man, his patience clearly drawing to an end, said, "Give me the gun."

"Over my dead body."

The most evil smile Juanita had ever seen on a human being monopolized the man's face. "I was hoping you'd say that." He lurched toward her.

Juanita started shooting.

"Say it again," Michael asked Billingsley, convinced her ears were playing tricks on her.

"You heard me right," Billingsley said. "There's no court for you today. The state is dropping the charges."

Michael stared.

"They captured the real killers," he added.

"How?"

"Your old neighbor, Juanita Perkins, caught them in her house—put a couple of holes in the big guy, but he'll live."

"Well, I'll be damned."

"It turns out that your ex-husband was involved in stealing a prototype for an experimental weapon from Initech. He'd been paid $1.4 million, but then he failed to deliver the package."

"One point four million? What did he do with the money? I never saw that kind of money."

"Apparently he had a Swiss account."

"Bastard! He cheated me on the divorce settlement."

Billingsley laughed. "I think it's more likely he was trying to hide it from the IRS."

"But I don't understand. Why would he do that? Steal?" She fell quiet. She knew why, didn't she?

Michael sighed. "When will I get out of here?"

"Soon. They're processing the paperwork now. It'll probably be around two o'clock. Then you're a free woman. Do you think you can hold on until then?"

"I think I'll be dancing a jig until then. Thank you," she said, tears leaking from her eyes. "Thank you so much."

"Don't thank me. Thank Juanita Perkins."

It was three o'clock when Michael finally tasted freedom. When she walked out of the jail, the whole Adams clan was there to greet her. All except her father and in a way he was there in spirit.

There were so many tears and hugs that she was overwhelmed by it all. One thing for sure, Michael never wanted to see the inside of a jail ever again.

"C'mon, we need to get you home," Sheldon

said, while Michael's gaggle of nieces and nephews swarmed around her. Even Donna approached with watery eyes and with Teddy on her hip. Having Donna's support through the whole ordeal finally bridged the gap between the two women. Michael finally accepted her in her heart as part of the family.

Flex opened his muscular arms and engulfed her in a hug that made it impossible to breathe. "Welcome home, sis. I've missed you bossing me around."

Michael smiled and laughed as he released her.

Peyton and Lincoln approached next, their new baby boy, Jackson Trey Carver, nestled in his mother's arms.

"Meet your new nephew," Peyton said through fat tears.

Michael took Jackson into her arms and cooed softly, "Welcome to the family."

"You might have another one on the way," Joey said from behind her.

Michael looked up at a beaming Joey and Ryan. "For real?"

Joey nodded. "I tested positive two days ago."

"Oh, that's wonderful." She slowly slid Jackson back into his mother's arms and then grabbed Joey in a fierce hug. "I'm so happy for you."

Too bad her father wasn't there to see this moment. Her heart grew heavy thinking about all the things she'd lost during this madness: her father, her freedom and even...

Michael lost her breath as her eyes snagged on the man across the street.

Kyson stood next to his car, watching her family mill about, hugging her.

Her heart soared at the sight of him while hope filled her head with possibilities. "Excuse me," she murmured, cutting through the family throng. "Let me through for a minute," she pleaded. "I'll be right back," she promised, and then looked both ways before crossing the street and racing up to Kyson.

When she stopped before him, she could barely see through the fat drops of her tears. "I can't believe you came."

"I guess I wanted to see you finally walk out of that place." He glanced down as if he didn't know what else to say.

"I want you to know that I'm truly sorry. I… I…" She allowed a moment of silence and then tried again. "I waited for this moment," she confessed. "I thought I knew what I wanted to say." Michael waited for him to look at her. When he didn't, she said, "Now I just wish that you would hold me."

The look on Kyson's face told her that wasn't possible.

Had she filled herself with false hope? Was it too late to bridge their differences?

"Why can't you look at me?" she asked.

"Look, Mike," he said. "I just wanted to congratulate you. I'm really happy you got out and all. I mean, it was looking pretty bad there for a moment."

"You don't have to tell me," she said in an attempt at humor.

"Well," he said, his eyes still averted, "I should go." He turned toward his car.

"Wait." She placed a hand against the door. "Just like that you're going to go? Why don't you come over to the house? I'm sure my family has a party all planned."

Kyson finally looked at her. "Look, Michael…" He hesitated. "You know, I also thought I knew what I'd say at this moment…but I don't."

"Say you'll come to the house—join the party."

He shook his head. "I'm not going to tell you that."

"But—"

"Michael, it can never work between the two of us."

"I didn't say—"

"It's what you're thinking. It's what I've been thinking. I care about you," he admitted. "A lot. More than a lot… I think I love you."

"Oh, Kyson…" She moved toward him, but he stepped back.

"Michael, whenever I ask myself whether I can truly build something with a woman I can't trust… the answer's no. I don't…*trust* you. There's no future if there's no trust."

"What do you mean?" She gasped. "I told you I

didn't have anything to do with Phil's death. I told you the truth about the kidnappers."

"And what about Phil being tied and gagged in the basement or the false statements you made at the station? You didn't tell me that Ray and Scott Damon kidnapped your ex-husband."

"It's not exactly something you blurt out." She tried to laugh.

He didn't. "Michael, you can't be honest just when it's convenient. You lied at your house, the station and even while lying in my bed."

She said nothing. She couldn't.

"I'm happy you're free, but as far as me and you…I just can't."

The lump in her throat was too large for her to swallow and the tears in her eyes were too thick to see through.

"Goodbye, Michael." He leaned forward, placed a feathery kiss against her lips. "I'm sorry." He opened his car door and climbed inside.

She stepped away in disbelief, watched him start the car and then pull into traffic and drive out of her life.

Chapter 31

Michael watched Kyson's car disappear into the distance. Her body trembled with despair while her heart shattered into a million pieces. "Don't go." Her words vanished into the wind.

Frankie approached. "Are you okay, Michael?"

She nodded, hoping to keep her emotions in check. Instead, when she turned toward her sisters, the truth tumbled out. "No," she croaked.

Frankie opened her arms in time for Michael to collapse in her embrace.

"I can't believe he left." Michael moaned pitifully. "What did I do? I messed up. I messed up bad."

"Shh, Mike. It's gonna be okay," Frankie soothed.

"No, it's not," Michael contradicted. "How can it be?"

"Yes, it will. You'll see," Frankie insisted. "C'mon. Let's get you home."

Michael allowed her sister to guide her back across the street to where the rest of the family had witnessed her heartbreak. No one said a word as loud, heart-wrenching sobs racked her body.

There was no party that night. When everyone piled into their childhood home, Michael almost immediately sought refuge in her old bedroom. She didn't feel like celebrating. How could she?

The man whom she'd hoped to have a second chance with had rejected her from his life—forever.

"Why don't you just get yourself some sleep," Sheldon suggested and then led her weeping sister into bed.

Michael curled in between the sheets while Sheldon, Frankie, Joey and Peyton helped tuck her in. Tears rained from her eyes, soaking her pillow.

"Try to get some sleep," Joey said, placing a kiss against her forehead.

Each sister murmured something more or less the same as they peppered their kisses along her forehead before filing out of the room. When they clicked off her light and left her to the darkness, Michael's tears and sobs increased.

"Kyson," she whispered. "I'm so sorry. Why won't you let me make it up to you?"

The responding silence crushed her spirit while flashes of the brief time she'd shared with Kyson replayed in her mind. Instantly, her body ached in remembrance of his touch, his taste, his everything.

She now knew what she'd lost. Kyson had been the one for her. She'd known the first time she'd laid eyes on him, the first times she'd kissed him and the first time that their bodies joined.

But they were a match doomed from the beginning. Why couldn't they have met under different circumstances? Why not at a store, a restaurant or a club? If given a chance, she would have done things so differently. She would've been completely honest and earned his trust, his heart, his love.

"Oh, God, make him change his mind," she prayed. "I'm so sorry. Please give me another chance. Please." Michael's eyelids grew heavy. Her pleas and tears exhausted her.

"Please give me another chance," she whispered drowsily. "Please. I want to do it all over…"

"Michael, wake up!"

"Please, God. Give me a second chance."

"Michael!" the voice persisted. "Wake up."

"Come back," Michael begged. "God, please make him come back."

"Michael," a chorus of voices insisted while hands rocked her body violently awake. "Michael, wake up."

"What?"

"I think she's delirious," Sheldon said, concerned.

Finally, Michael's eyes fluttered open, but the piercing light from the ceiling fixture stabbed her brain like a rusty dagger. She quickly slammed her eyes closed again. "Please turn off that light," she croaked.

"Well, at least she's still alive," Joey said with a note of sarcasm.

"Why are you yelling?" Michael asked, her mouth a big cotton ball.

The girls chuckled above her.

"That's what you get for trying to drink the Damon twins under the table," Frankie said.

"What?" Michael struggled to sit up. "Shut off that damn light," she commanded again.

One of the girls hit the switch.

"Here. Drink this." Peyton shoved a hot tomato drink to her mouth.

Michael gagged. "Ugh. What is that?"

"Linc's famous remedy for a hangover," Peyton said.

"It's horrible," Michael croaked, attempting to open her eyes again. When she did, she blinked in confusion. "What the hell are you doing still pregnant?"

"Trust me. I wonder that every time I wake up, too." P.J. laughed. "Nobody is more anxious than me to have this baby."

Michael glanced down and saw her mismatched

polka-dot and plaid pajamas. It then occurred to her that she wasn't in her old childhood bedroom, but her bed at her new home. "I don't understand. What day is it?"

"Oh, yeah." Sheldon shook her head. "You had way too much to drink."

"Whatever. Here." Peyton shoved something into her hands.

"What's this?"

"A bill. I had to get the backseat of my car cleaned since you felt the need to unload your dinner back there."

Just thinking about vomiting made Michael's stomach lurch; she peeled out of the sheets and raced toward the bathroom where she emptied what was left in her stomach.

"Oh, good Lord." Sheldon's maternal instincts kicked in and she prepared a cool washcloth for Michael's head.

"Why am I so sick? We didn't have a party last night."

"We sure the hell did. You drank and partied until the Peppermill closed," Sheldon said. "How could you forget? We were celebrating your divorce."

"But that would mean…" Michael slumped against the tiled bathroom floor and leaned back against the tub. "It couldn't have been a dream. It was too…real. Phil was murdered and—"

"Oh, God," Frankie said, rolling her eyes. "There

she goes again. Mike, you've got to stop that. If something was to happen you'd feel horrible. I know this may sound harsh, but honey, it's time to move on."

"He's alive?"

"Don't sound so shocked," Peyton said. "You're making me nervous."

Michael couldn't wrap her brain around what her sisters were saying. "What about Daddy?"

"What about him?"

"Is he all right? He's still alive, too?"

The girls looked at one another.

"Maybe she has alcohol poisoning," Joey suggested. "We should get her to a hospital."

"No. No," Michael croaked, her gaze falling to the floor. "I'm fine…I guess." She pressed the cool towel back against her face. "It was all a dream," she said with a`note of disbelief. "You were all there. Even that godawful Juanita Perkins was there."

"That old lady leading that crazy Neighborhood Watch group at your old place?" Sheldon asked. "Hell, that sounds more like a nightmare."

Michael bobbed her head. "It was."

The Damon twins hadn't kidnapped Phil.

They hadn't shoved him into the car, tied and gagged him and put him in her basement.

A psycho Bonnie and Clyde hadn't killed Phil and his new girlfriend—did he have a new girlfriend?

Her father was alive. Thank God.

At last, her brain seized on another image. "But he'd seemed so real…"

Epilogue

Marlin and Donna's one-year anniversary was a joyous celebration. Cloistered together in the back of Nicolino's, the Adams clan laughed, joked and shared stories of how Joey's husband, Ryan, had crashed their wedding and had mistaken Joey for the bride to be.

Michael surprised everyone by buying their father and Donna tickets for a luxury cruise. "I figured you'd enjoy it since you didn't get a chance to take a honeymoon," she said, beaming at the happy couple.

Tears sprang into Donna's eyes and she reached over and hugged Michael. Everyone else at the table just stared, wide-eyed.

"Okay," P.J. said, leaning over. "Who are you and what have you done with my sister?"

"What? Can't I be nice to my father and stepmother?" Her comment didn't stop the stares, but honestly she was starting to get used to them.

In the last few days, Michael's transformation had been as dramatic as Ebenezer Scrooge's. What surprised everyone the most was her change toward her ex-husband. No longer bitter about the failure of her marriage, Michael decided that it was time to move on.

Sure, she might be single again, but for some reason her heart held out strong hope for the future. Sure, she still wanted to belong to someone, but for the first she realized it was more important to be with the *right* one.

"Buon compleanno! Buon compleanno!"

Michael turned at the sound of a group of people singing. Toward the restaurant's bar, a group of waiters and waitresses surrounded a table.

"It must be someone's birthday," Joey commented.

Michael nodded through a pang of déjà vu. "Excuse me for a moment," she said absently, and stood up from her chair.

"Mike, where are you going?" someone asked.

She didn't answer, she couldn't. She waded across the restaurant, trying to get a better view of the surrounded table, but the servers launched into a second chorus and she drifted toward the bar so she could wait.

Move out of the way, her brain screamed, anxious to sate its curiosity.

Finally she got her wish as the crowd parted.

Michael sucked in a sharp breath when her eyes landed on a man she had only seen in her dreams. Skin the color of dark chocolate, hard muscles bulging along his shoulders and arms. He was just the way she'd envisioned him to be.

The stranger looked up. He caught her stare, cocked his head and smiled.

"It can't be," she whispered.

The man said something to his male companion and stood up from his table. As he approached, Michael's stomach twisted into knots while her throat constricted painfully.

"Excuse me, miss," he said in a voice she'd know anywhere. "But have we met?"

Michael swallowed. "I—I don't think so," she said softly.

"Are you sure?" he persisted. "I very rarely forget a face."

She smiled.

"Or a smile," he added.

"No," she said. "I think I'd remember you."

His smile took her breath away. "Well," he said, looking up to see the bar, "it may be my birthday, but would you mind if I bought *you* a drink?"

"I would mind," she said, loosening up. "I should buy you a drink."

He sat on the stool next to her. "Before you do that, let me introduce myself. My name is Kyson Dekker, and you?"

Her heart took flight. "Michael...Michael Adams."

She watched his eyes twinkle as they roamed over her. "Well, Michael. I'm pleased to meet you..."

USA TODAY BESTSELLING AUTHOR

BRENDA JACKSON

IRRESISTIBLE FORCES

Taylor Steele wants a baby, not a relationship. So she
proposes a week of mind-blowing sex in the Caribbean
to tycoon Dominic Saxon, whose genes seem perfect.
No strings—just mutual enjoyment. But when it's over,
will either of them be able to say goodbye?

"Brenda Jackson has written another sensational novel...
stormy, sensual and sexy—all the things a romance reader
could want in a love story."
—*Romantic Times BOOKreviews* on *Whispered Promises*

*Coming the first week of May
wherever books are sold.*

KIMANI™
ROMANCE

www.kimanipress.com   KPBJ0640508

Book #1 in

THE THREE MRS. FOSTERS

THIS
TIME FOR
GOOD

FAVORITE AUTHOR

CARMEN
GREEN

About to lose her family business because of her late
husband's polygamy, Alexandria accepts Hunter's help.
But she's not letting any man run her life—
not even one who sets her senses aflame.

"Ms. Green sweeps the reader away on the lush carpet
of reality-grounded romantic fantasy."
—*Romantic Times BOOKreviews* on *Commitments*

*Coming the first week of May
wherever books are sold.*

KIMANI™
ROMANCE

www.kimanipress.com   KPCG0650508

Down and out...but not really

Indiscriminate Attraction

ESSENCE BESTSELLING AUTHOR

Linda Hudson-Smith

Searching the streets and homeless shelters for his missing
twin, shabbily disguised Chad Kingston accepts volunteer
Laylah Versailles's help. Luscious Laylah's determination
to turn "down-and-out" Chad's life around has a heated
effect on him. But Chad's never trusted women—
and Laylah has secrets.

"Hudson-Smith does an outstanding job...
A truly inspiring novel!"
—*Romantic Times BOOKreviews* on *Secrets & Silence*

*Coming the first week of May
wherever books are sold.*

KIMANI™
ROMANCE

her kind of

Man

Favorite author
PAMELA YAYE

As a gawky teen, Makayla Stevens yearned for
Kenyon Blake. Now he's the uncle of one of her students,
and wants to get better acquainted with Makayla.
The reality is even hotter than her teenage fantasies.
But their involvement could damage her career…
and her peace of mind.

"*Other People's Business*…is a fun and lighthearted story…
an entertaining novel."
—*Romantic Times BOOKreviews* on
Pamela Yaye's debut novel

*Coming the first week of May
wherever books are sold.*

KIMANI
ROMANCE

www.kimanipress.com

KPPY0670508

Her dreams of love came true...twice.

ESSENCE BESTSELLING AUTHOR

DONNA
HILL

Charade

Betrayed by Miles Bennett, the first man she'd let into her heart, Tyler Ellington flees to Savannah where she falls for photographer Sterling Grey. Sterling is everything Miles is not...humorous, compassionate, honest. But when she returns to New York, Tyler is yet again swayed by Miles's apologies and passion. Now torn between two men, she must decide which love is the real thing.

"A lighthearted comedy, rich in flavor and unpredictable in story, *Divas, Inc.* proves how limitless this author's talent is."
—*Romantic Times BOOKreviews*

*Coming the first week of May
wherever books are sold.*

ARABESQUE®

www.kimanipress.com   KPDH1010508